Gloriously LOST

DEEPTHI SRINIVAS

INDIA • SINGAPORE • MALAYSIA

ISBN 979-8-89026-828-0

To our precious amma, Late Srimati Padmavathi

CHAPTER 1

Chennai

The tides from the sea reflected the noon sun, not missing a ray. Samantha's body sunk in the middle of a soft mattress in a hotel-like dormitory maintained by the Hope hospitals. The room was deserted, and erratic noises of the wind, fan, and birds broke into her head. Minor jerks traveled from her toes, across her fingers to her eyes, leaving her face to frown. Her eyes shifted hurriedly under tight eyelids and were soon relaxed by the sound of sea waves from far away.

She clenched the bedsheet forcing herself to open her eyes and did so only with a narrow slit. She looked at a black fan fixed on a white ceiling, and passed on to a glass lamp with a silver flowered pattern opposite her bed against a grey wall, under which there was a cushioned couch made of black fabric. It replicated a bedroom of a three-star hotel with a few luxurious interior elements. She tried to raise herself up slightly, pressing her lips tight, and noticed a succulent with long snake-like leaves beside the couch, followed by a door to the balcony next to it. The plant looked neatly maintained with no dried edges or fallen leaves. She was sure that she had never been to this place before in her whole life.

Samantha flinched, holding her head tightly at the temples. It felt like she had been banged by a hammer. She strained her red-veined eyes, squinting and struggling to look beyond the balcony. She stared at the horizon, amazed and confused at the same time. The sight of the sea made her heart rumble. As far as she could remember, she had lived in Bangalore since her childhood.

'Beach in Bangalore?' she mumbled. She was debilitated enough that she could not even lift herself up. The only face she wanted to see at that moment was her mother's. Tears rolled across her cheeks out of the growing fear, the fear of being lost.

'Maa-a,' she tried calling out with her broken voice. She sounded different; her throat was pitch dry and her words mostly choked. She felt hollow inside, like a lost fish in a deep sea. 'Maa,' she cried once again.

She heard footsteps approaching her. Her bubble of hope burst instantly with the arrival of a nurse rushing into the room. She again tried to raise her torso and could lift only a few inches from the bed. Right after the nurse, Andrew came running into the room wearing his doctor's coat. He was explicitly astonished to find Samantha awake after a long 28 hours of sedation. He quickly aided a hand of support looking at her and trying to move.

'Get some water, quick!' he instructed the nurse, his arms wrapped over Samantha's shoulders. Samantha shuddered out of protest, trying to stabilize herself. The nurse poured some water into a tall crystal glass, spilling most of it, and handed it to Samantha with trembling hands. Her mind was alarmed that the girl who was unconscious for almost one and half days and was rumored to create a nuisance was finally awake. Samantha wiped her tears clumsily and grabbed the glass from the nurse. She gulped the water, choking on it.

'Slow. Slow.' Andrew stroked her back.

She loved the water at that moment. She felt the path it took to reach her stomach, cooling as it went. She felt her body rejuvenate, but that didn't make her feel any better to be found in an unknown place. She sighed after her last sip was down. She looked at the doctor with hundreds of questions running in her head, but only uttered, 'Mumma.'

'Oh, no-no. You're okay. Your parents are not here. It's just a small injury. You're absolutely fine.'

How can a girl be okay in an unknown place with strangers knowing her parents aren't there? She could not say that out loud. 'Maa!' she screamed out in a broken voice instead.

'Nothing to worry about. Your parents are not here. It's just you.' His response terrified her. She imagined herself running out of that place, escaping these people.

She stared at Andrew for a brief moment and cried out louder, choking with tears.

'Easy, Sam, please calm down.' He gave mild strokes to her back to subside her heavy panting. Out of this complete turmoil, Samantha could not help but notice the one familiar thing about her: her name. She squinted her eyes and looked at Andrew in an attempt to recognize him, to remember anything from the previous night, although she could not remember one thing. Every time Samantha needed a doctor, whether it be a fever, catching a cold, stomach upset, or an injury at school, it was always the same doctor who treated her. Samantha recalled Dr. Murthy and could see him vividly. However, the one beside her did not have Dr. Murthy's thick glasses and pouched belly. He looked like how Dr. Murthy would look in his twenties, or much better. She wondered what made her parents change the family consultation from Dr. Murthy to this random one.

'Nurse, one minute.' Andrew gestured for her to take care of Samantha. He walked out into the hallway grabbing his phone from his pocket. Mrs. Layla's contact number topped his frequently dialed list. His trembling thumb dabbed firmly on her name. She picked up the call within a couple of rings. 'Andrew! What happened, did she wake up?'

'Hi, Ma'am. Nothing to worry about. Samantha is completely alright. She just gained consciousness.'

'Oh, thank God.'

'Yea. But…'

'But, what?'

'She keeps asking for you. I think she'll feel better if you talk to her.'

'Me? I…I don't know, Andrew. What if she...if she wails?'

'No! Trust me, nothing of that sort will happen this time. She...she seems to miss you.'

Silence came from the other end.

'Ma'am, you there?'

'Yes, yes. Are you sure, Andrew? Because, if you remembered the last time....'

'I'm sure, Ma'am. She is genuinely asking for you. I will get her on the line right away.'

He ran into the room while Samantha was still crying. 'Sam, someone wants to talk to you. Here.' He placed the phone over her ear.

Samantha held her breath and listened carefully. She heard a voice which had the power to wipe off all her sorrows. The voice that could give her hope for life, even on her deathbed.

Her mother spoke, 'Hello. Sam?' Samantha's heart melted. She could not stop tears flowing, only this time out of happiness. The voice from the phone reassured her identity. Words trembled to slip out of her throat. She murmured, 'Maa. Maa, where are you? Please come soon, I am so scared. I don't know where I am.'

'Oh! My baby, don't cry. There is nothing to be scared of. You're in safe hands. Andrew. Andrew will take care of you. And I'll be on my way.'

'Ma, please take me home. I don't want to be here. Please,' she almost screamed.

'Sam, I'm sorry that I'm not there with you right now. But, listen, Pappa and I will be there soon. And we all can come back home. Please listen to Andrew till then. Stay strong, alright?'

Samantha nodded in relief. She controlled her breath and tried to breathe coherently. *When will you come,* she wanted to ask. She prepared herself and said, 'When...' after a few moments but realized she could hear nothing on the other line. She was totally upset by the silence. She stared at the phone as if it were the phone's fault. Andrew took it back and found Mrs. Layla had hung up. He tried calling her again but failed to connect. 'Might be a bad network,' he shrugged.

Samantha was partially convinced by her mother's words to stay in this unknown place until she was reconnected with her parents.

Later that day, Layla called Andrew again. He answered the call immediately although he was in the middle of a consultation at the hospital.

'You were right, Andrew. I sense a lot of difference in her. We are planning to come and pick her up.'

'What?' He smirked. 'Ma'am, I think you're mistaken. She is alright now. That doesn't mean she can be exposed to that environment again. Please give me some time to keep her in observation. We decided this before.'

'Yes, I understand that. We did make a decision. But look at her, from throwing stuff at us and running away from the hospital to now wanting to be with us. Isn't that progress?'

'True. It is progress, but not a sustainable one. This is an unbelievable shift in her mood and we need to keep her in observation. Ma'am, please. I understand your feelings. But, I'm sure we can't manage if she goes missing once again.'

Deep silence filled a few moments.

'Alright.' Her voice was stiff, ' Please take care of her. Let us know her progress. Thank you once again for your help.' She hung up.

Andrew took a deep sigh, looking at the vast spread of sea out the window, preparing himself for whatever he had signed up for.

CHAPTER 2

Two nurses, wearing blue surgical caps hesitantly peer into the room I am in. One enters first, who I recognize gave me a glass of water earlier. She forcefully pulls in another hand behind her, revealing the entire body of someone who clearly did not want to participate. They both walk toward me with erect bodies, which partially looks robotic. One of them takes a syringe and a sealed glass bottle from the tray that is kept right by the entrance to the room. She throws an indifferent look at me; I do not understand the intention behind it as half of her face is covered with a mask of the same color as her cap.

She approaches me and says, 'Stretch your hand please.' I see a loaded injection in her hand and do not want to really go through that. I have never preferred an injection in my entire life. I stare at the injection she held, not knowing how to avoid it. 'Your hand please?' she insists.

'Why? Why do I need to take it?' I ask, gathering some courage.

'It's part of your medication.' Her voice stays firm and indifferent. "Neethu" the tag on her dress reads. I see a shadow slowly cast upon Neethu's face. I slightly turn and there is the other nurse. She takes position behind me. Her name tag reads 'Preethi'. I'm quite unsure if the nervousness I'm feeling currently is because of the injection or the nurses closing in.

'It's okay. It won't hurt,' the nurse at the back assures me. *No, it's not okay.* Although the tone was convincing, I'm sure I do not want to take that damn injection. 'No. I...' *Why can't I say these sentences as I think?* ' I don't want to–'

'Let them, Sam.' A man's voice cuts in, giving me shivers. 'You need this now,' he says, walking toward me. *Who are you,* I wonder. 'Andrew' his name tag reads. Mumma's words ring in my head. "Listen to Andrew till I come." My hand extends automatically, without a second thought. The nurse rubs my arm with a small ball of cotton in no time. *This indeed did not hurt.*

*

When I was left behind at the school by the van, you had not trusted the uncle from the next street who offered to drop me home. You'd insisted I stay at the school until dad came to pick me up.

When my Math teacher offered home tuition for me along with the other students, you'd declined it saying Simon would take care of it. I for sure knew that you did not trust the teacher being a male.

When I took a car after my exam to come home on my own, you'd lectured me for making such a decision, which threatened your worst fear of being the mother of a young girl.

What made you believe these people? This doctor. This place. How were you convinced to leave me here? I really wanna know, Ma…I do.

CHAPTER 3

If a daughter is sedated due to a drug overdose and has been unconscious for almost one and a half days, any mother would be shattered and would run to the daughter whatever the situation might be. The relationship between Samantha and her mother was like any other mother and daughter until Simon died, or rather before Samantha could hit her parents and escape from the hospital twice.

Samantha used to share everything with her mother, from funny moments in college to her beauty problems, gossip, food cravings, the small changes in her body and the lingerie she needed to choose, her view on politics, parenting, the education system, career, and even complaints about her brother, Simon.

Layla also used to be a mother with reasonable expectations like her daughter's attention on weekends, her company while shopping, teaching her to cook, her doing well on exams, to inform wherever she goes out with friends, and not getting into habits like drinking or smoking, to take care of herself, to be her only princess.

But all this changed a year ago. Samantha stopped being a normal daughter to her parents as soon as she found out her brother's funeral was held without her. Her brother, Simon, was six years older than her. He took care of her closely, right from her education, attended PTA meetings since he moved to college, took her shopping, taught her how to dress, to ride a bike, and expected her to have a vision and goal for life and not to live leisurely. Simon had played many roles in Samantha's life in addition to being a brother; he was her best friend, a guide, a guard, a role model, and also an enemy, sometimes. Her parents had always tried to console her by stating the fact that she had been also hurt physically and was admitted to the hospital when he passed, which she never accepted to be enough to have missed her brother's funeral. After all, Mr. and Mrs. Victor had also lost their only son.

*

Samantha felt surreal to have found herself in such a situation. Her head hurt as if a nail hammered at the center of her skull. She squeezed her eyes shut, reached her head, and pressed the temples with her fingertips, trying to resolve the mystery of how she got into this unknown place. Her eyes pictured only darkness. She stayed quiet in spite of having a ton of questions arise within her. She was ready to obey whatever Andrew had to say in order to get back home as per her mother's words.

'You must be wondering how we found you,' Andrew said, wanting to explain everything to her. 'Well…'

Samantha blinked, having no idea what he was talking about. Her mind was blank. 'Found me?' She frowned. *I was thinking,* she thought, *my parents had sent me here.*

'Yeah. I went in search of you to all the possible places. You did give a challenge this time unlike the first.' He smirked. 'I finally found you on the top of that old building. And when I tried to rescue you, that guy, your friend, pulled you down the stairs and unfortunately you stumbled down and got hurt.' Neither a friend nor a building came to her mind. She could only remember vivid glimpses from her childhood like it happened yesterday. A watermelon challenge she and her brother used to play every summer. She recalled Simon chugging his seven pieces of watermelon within a few minutes and taking a fair share of hers as well. Everything she could remember felt like they were from a different lifetime.

'He just collapsed.' Andrew continued his explanation in the most convincing tone, 'He was already out of his senses, and on top of that he was mad at me. Don't worry, I've admitted him to the hospital and brought you here. I put you in an ambulance and managed till we reached Chennai. Before you say anything, this is not a hospital. I mean partially connected, but I'm sure you'll not feel like you're at one. Trust me. This is just for a few weeks. We'll be back within no time. Okay?'

Samantha's face was furrowed in absolute uncertainty.

'What happened?' he asked her. 'Sam, are you listening to me?'

She frowned as she spoke, 'I believe you're confusing me with someone else. I don't remember any of that.'

Andrew's eyes widened; he felt disoriented for a moment. 'Oh, right.' *Of course,* he thought, *cocaine is capable of doing this, and more.* 'By the way, how did you get out of that hospital?' he curiously asked.

'Which hospital?' The calmness in her tone, the confidence in defending that it wasn't her who he was talking about, the disconnect to the outer world from her thoughts. That very moment, he knew this was not the person he had known for the past half-year.

*

The late evening sky, the breeze that was carried from the middle of the sea, the smell of fresh air, and the tiny sparkles of light from ships that traveled across the sea, all made Samantha feel lighter. She stared at the starry sky for hours recalling the best moments she had spent with her family when she was younger. The quarrels she'd had with her mother, the pampering of her father, the bets with her brother. Some made her giggle while others made her cry. That night, Samantha relived many of her joyous moments in retrospect, her heart filled with nostalgia.

Everything was under control until an unbearable throbbing filled her ears. She ground her teeth enduring the head-churning pain. She panted. Her vision lost control. She pressed her face against the pillow, forcing herself to sleep. Going from dim to bright, she saw lights spread all over and fill her vision. She blinked hard several times to focus beyond the light. Her untied hair fluttered all across her face due to the wind.

She found herself running in the middle of a two-lane main road amongst passing vehicles. She ran against the fast-paced cars and trucks, dodging one after the other. She gasped for breath, her face turned red partially due to the headlights and the rest due to her racing heart. She saw the silhouette of a tall man standing on the divider a little far away making gestures to run fast and move towards him. Samantha ran faster towards the silhouette in order to reach him; she got closer and felt as though she recognized the person.

A beam of headlight fell on the profile of the silhouette and she knew that it was her brother. She ran with a wide smile and teary eyes, stretching her hands toward him. The moment Samantha felt the tip of her brother's fingers, he was hit by a truck and crashed his head against the road. Samantha halted with her breath struck, eyes wide, whispering 'no' as she exhaled. Her face was illuminated with the scattering of various headlights from vehicles speeding by, her head weighed multiple tons that she couldn't bear. She heard multiple honks at a time in discord. She finally decided to approach her brother's body with trembling limbs. She put her right foot forward when a bright beam simultaneously headed towards her, blinding her vision.

Samantha rolled across her bed and collapsed on the floor. The nightmare had startled her and she found herself on the ground with an aching hip. She got herself together without a cry. She suspected the nurse from the other room might have heard her falling off the cot but there was slight snoring she could hear. She felt terrible. She wiped the sweating face with the center of her palm and lied down on the bed, haunted by the dream.

A day passed within a blink. Andrew visited the dorm the next morning. He wore a pale pink shirt and dark blue pants; he wasn't wearing his doctor's coat this time. He entered hastily as if a patient in an emergency ward were waiting for him, but still with grace. He always walked like that. 'Good morning, Doctor!' Neethu said, getting up from her chair. Her eyes gazed at him all over in admiration. A smile visited his face for a quick second.

'Morning. Did Sam take tablets last night?'

'No, Doctor. I insisted but...'

'Alright. Let me check.' He walked straight to Samantha who was sitting on a wooden seat in the balcony corner, her arms resting on the metal fence that surrounded the balcony area. She wore a white T-shirt and black joggers, which were different from the blue patient clothes she'd worn the previous day. Andrew had arranged a set of casual clothes for Samantha with help of Neethu.

'Good morning, Sam. looking great today!' His voice bore great energy. She glanced at Andrew with a firm face for a moment and turned back to continue looking at the vehicles passing by the main road below. Her look was indifferent. 'How are you today?' he asked his regular question, expecting an answer in return. She stayed put. 'Did you take your tablets yesterday? She stayed grim with no response.

'Hey, listen, you need to take your tablets every day.' He waved the medicine sheets in front of her face like magic cards. 'This will regulate your brain activity, and give you some peace and good sleep. These are essential to you now. You know what I mean?' He tried to look into her eyes. None of his words seemed to enter her wandering head. She was terrified by the nightmare so much that it lingered no matter what she did. Samantha cursed herself for having such an awful dream, although dreams are not under one's control. The dream added up to the million questions she already had regarding her present situation. She wanted to see her brother, touch his hands and his face, hug him and make sure he was all okay.

'Is everything okay?' Andrew shook her by her shoulder, 'Listen, you're going to be fine. You need not worry so much. You will meet your family once this course of observation is completed. I think you can give yourself some leisure till then, right?'

She extremely missed her parents and wanted to share her agony with them right at that moment. Her loneliness craved some tears to accompany her. Samantha looked beyond the sea with a sigh. She remembered screaming,

"I hate you all. I've got the worst family ever," when she was not allowed to go on a school trip with her friends. She recalled how she wished to have lived alone. *No. No.* She shook her head and pressed her eyelids closed, spilling some tears. *I'm sorry for what I've done. I cannot tell y'all how much I love you. I probably would've never told you. I miss you, Ma. I miss you, Papa. I miss you, Bunny. Please take me back with you.*

Andrew stopped talking and let her sink into the little bubble of memories.

CHAPTER 4

I have died every day waiting for you... sang the audio in the car. Despite the song being melodious and soothing to the soul, the volume hurt her head. Samantha sat in the front passenger seat pushing herself against the car door, intimidated. The streets looked clean, and decorated beautifully with plants along the pathway.

They arrived at the hospital in five minutes. Andrew quickly got down and opened the door on Samantha's side, extending his hand for support which she refused. They climbed the steps and passed across the silver piped glass doors. A few steps after the glass door, right opposite the reception, was a two-foot-tall statue of Lord Ganesha elevated on a concrete pillar. The place looked divine with colorful flowers and incense sticks.

'Excuse me. Is Dr. Vishnu in?' He barged into a conversation of two receptionists.

'Yes, Doctor. Third floor, his room.'

Andrew and Dr. Vishnu discussed Samantha's activities and couldn't come to a conclusion verbally. Followed by a couple of tests and an injection, Samantha was sent into the PET scanner. While the procedure took about thirty minutes, she couldn't avoid recalling the water ride she enjoyed on a school trip to the theme park, where she was sent through a huge tube that led to the pool underneath.

'Please wait here.' Andrew pointed at the never-ending row of metal seats outside the doctor's room after the PET scan.

The neurologist stared at the scan for quite some time, altering the lights on either side of the scan.

'You see, the greenish and yellowish dots on the temporal lobe area?' Dr. Vishnu pointed at the scan placed on the LED.

'Yeah?' Andrew hunched forward on the chair and stared, following where the doctor pointed.

'I strongly think there might have been a brain stroke or an injury that has caused rapid activity. This intense activity of the brain only happens at high pressure that presses on the region which controls memory. The scan shows that the temporal lobe is affected, which might be when she had fallen. This might have affected the memory of the girl.' The doctor lifted his head up, adjusting his glasses.

Andrew jerked forward. 'Are you sure? Do you think she forgot everything? Wait, that can't be the case...She asked for her mother as soon as she woke up.'

'We can't be sure of that yet, Doctor. The effect might be severe since she had drug consumption at the time of injury. You'll need to have a talk with her to find out.'

*

Samantha sat on the cold metal chair outside the doctor's room. She was alone, despite being surrounded by various patients and hospital staff. She saw herself as a kid who was being pampered by her whole family.

"No, don't do it alone," her mother used to tell every time she tried to boil milk for herself.

"Take your brother along." Her father used to protect her every time she stepped out for an errand.

"I'm right here." Her brother used to assure her every time she was stared at by a stranger.

What made them leave me alone here, in this unknown place? How did they think that I can manage this alone? I am now at the most insecure place in my life and you guys are not around. What have I done, Mumma, why are you not with me now? Samantha damned herself.

*

This was not the first time Samantha felt isolated from the rest of the world.

She was brought home from the hospital only a couple of days after Simon had died. Samantha slowly walked into the living room. The scent of the garlands that were placed on Simon's body the previous day seemed to have infused into the walls of the house. She entered the house knowing it is going to be one person less occupied, one person less noisy, and one person less from her definition of the word family since she had known one.

The first thing that occurred to her was to retrieve her brother and fix this broken piece of heart as if it that were possible. After a moment she realized that the reality was highly contradicting compared to her idea. She had missed seeing the face of her brother for the last time ever, as all the funeral formalities were done by the time she was brought home. She felt betrayed. She stepped slowly into the hallway reaching Simon's picture placed on the wooden table with garlands and a lighted candle in front. Her house was filled with people who gathered to convey their condolences for the third-day ceremony.

She burst within herself not knowing whom to complain to for not holding back her brother, for not trying to wake her up from unconsciousness, for not coming home a day prior. She collapsed at the wooden table, not able to stand. Her mother was sitting on the couch surrounded by a few ladies, she was not in a position to talk or even notice that her one and only daughter had arrived home. Her father was standing in one corner of the living room with three of his friends around. The rest were conversing about what a perfect son Simon was. Samantha knew more than what those people spoke. She knew how Simon gave his fullest as a student, as an employee, as a son, and as a brother. Samantha felt devastated knowing she couldn't see her brother again.

Mr. Murthy, who was one of Victor's good friends, entered with his family. They conveyed their condolences to Victor first and then to Layla. 'It's highly unfortunate, Victor, I'm sorry for the great loss!' he said. His words crushed Samantha more. *Yes, Uncle, yes. Yes. Yes. This is a loss that cannot be regained or re-earned. A loss for my entire life. Forever!* She wanted to scream. Despite many people visiting them that evening, no one spoke to Samantha, no one asked how she was or how she felt. People who visited, including her parents, thought Simon's death would not have affected a girl who had just finished college. That it would pass on as any other event in her life. On the other hand, Samantha was undergoing a heartbreak that had no healing.

The worst thing is to avoid a person not knowing that those were their last few days. It had been a week since Samantha had spoken to her brother as usual. She had avoided him in every way possible. She did not wish him good mornings, did not eat when he was at the table, she didn't even talk about him with her mother or father. The guilt of how she'd acted made her feel small. Her throat hurt, heart grew heavier. She wanted a shoulder to cry on, a person to confess all her mistakes. At that very moment, she felt isolated from this whole world with many people around her but none to speak with.

CHAPTER 5

His heart pounded louder in rhythm with the "ring ring" that was banging in his ears. The call was picked up within five rings.

'Hi, Andrew. Is everything okay?'

'Yes, Ma'am. I just called you to inform you about something important.'

'Okay?'

'Please, don't panic.'

'Well, you asking me not to panic is actually panicking. What is it? Is my daughter okay?'

"What's wrong? Gimme the phone." Andrew heard Victor's telephonic voice from behind.

'Well, the other day…'

'Which day? Andrew, just tell us. What's the matter?'

Andrew noticed that his forehead was already sweating. He took a deep breath before talking.

'The other day, when I rescued Samantha from that old building, there was a slight push and pull that happened between me and her friend. I'm referring to the tall guy.'

'I'm aware. Go on…'

'Yeah. But…'

'I'm listening.'

'I found Sam a little… little ignorant about things and took a brain scan today. Just a general check-up. The doctor says she might have minor memory loss.'

There was a gasp and mumbling from the other end.

'WHAT? HOW?' Victor screamed.

'Sir, the thing is, when I was carrying her down the stairs, that guy pushed me and eventually she fell. She might've hit her head slightly against the wall. It did not look serious at that time. The doctor says that as she was already on a high dose of drugs, that the minor hit would've affected her memory. But trust me, I have seen cases as such in the past and they have recovered in just weeks. You really need not worry about this much.'

'Andrew. Andrew. If you had a daughter, would you not be worried in a situation like this? What are you even talking about not worrying?' Victor fumed.

'Yes, sir. I would If I were left clueless. And I don't want to leave you at that. Trust me. Please.'

Andrew left a few seconds of silence to let his words seep in and continued to talk. 'On the brighter side, she did not get any outbursts till now. She did not shout, did not hurt anyone. I believe it's because she doesn't remember all that happened. She only looks like a little girl who is away from her family.'

Victor signed. 'How are we going to fix this, Andrew?'

His words echoed in Andrew's ears for quite some time.

*

The balcony of Samantha's room captured half of the horizon. She has gotten used to waking up to the coos of pigeons behind the windows, the caws of crows from the balcony, the endless honking from highways far away, and a little of Andrew too.

Samantha spent the whole time isolated, staring at the sea over the balcony. The dorm led to the beach if one crossed the two-way road that was right below the building. Andrew visited every day. His prime time till midafternoon was spent at the hospital and the rest with Samantha. He would wish her good mornings, ask if she had slept well, enquire about how she felt, and would plead to eat whenever it was time for a meal. Samantha ate her first meal only on the second day, and nothing otherwise. He would spend most of the time walking around, making her bed, staring at Samantha whilst she gazed somewhere else. Andrew was not going to force her on anything that could spoil the peace she has in solitude. But he knew exactly what to do in order to give her mental peace.

The following morning, he took her to the meditation hall which was located on the top floor of the dormitory. The space was wide enough to fit almost thirty people at a time for a session. The front of the hall was attached with a mirror that covered the entire wall. Both sides were decorated with beautiful succulents, giving the place a healthy look.

Andrew pulled out a yoga mat from one of the cupboards. 'Please sit.' he said, spreading it out on the floor graciously. Samantha obeyed. Andrew also sat on the floor along with her 'Have you meditated before?'

Samantha's eyebrows raised spontaneously to his question, she shook her head slowly without spilling a word.

'Follow as I say. First, sit straight.' He straightened his torso as he said this, while she sat up making the slightly curved torso straight. 'Good. close your eyes now.'

Samantha blinked, hesitating. 'Try closing them for a minute. I will close mine as well,' he said. 'You can open your eyes whenever you feel uncomfortable.'

She slowly gathered her upper and lower eyelids together.

'Take a deep breath. This is inhale. Do this for the count of four. And exhale. Inhale. And exhale as long as you can. A couple more times.' Samantha followed his instructions without a question. 'Now tell me what are all the sounds you can hear?'

She spoke, while her eyelids fluttered. 'You. I can hear you. The pigeons and…' She strained her eyes pushing the eyelids close together before she could concentrate further. She heard the honking of vehicles from far away. 'Cars…on the roads.'

'Good.' Andrew opened his eyes and looked at Samantha's tensed face. Her face was frowned upon and sweaty. Her eyes struggled under the tightly pressed lids.

'Relax. Stay calm. Open your eyes, Sam. Are you okay?' Samantha's eyes were red-veined and she breathed hard.

'What happened? Easy. Easy.'

Samantha was not ready to tell him exactly why she felt the way she did as soon as she heard the honking.

*

She thought about nothing. Her head was completely void and she only blinked occasionally. Andrew entered making sure not to disturb the peacefulness of the room. Samantha sat on the couch cast by the initial rays of dusk. Andrew sat next to her with a Rubik's cube in his hand.

'Hey, you okay?'

She gave a slight nod.

'What happened this morning? What startled you?' He waited against her insusceptible silence and continued talking. 'Because that helps me understand what exactly is happening, and if anything sounds unusual, we have the opportunity to act upon it as soon as possible. You know what I mean?' Her gaze did not sway from the sea.

Andrew continued to speak, twisting the top and bottom sections of the cube effortlessly with his fingertips. 'Alright. Sam, look, isn't it pretty? See, here we've got white at the center, which means this side has to be sorted with white.' He turned the cube a little and said, 'here the centre is red, so this is the red side. Are you getting it, Sam?' he asked, turning to her face. He looked in her eyes, expecting a response at least once. He sighed.

'I...' He paused hearing the door open; it was the nurse. He adjusted, made his voice brisk knowing the nurse's presence, and spoke, 'I'll keep this here, near the books. You can try it at your leisure. I mean... if you want to. There are even a few interesting books. I—'

' Hi, Andrew,' the nurse said gaily.

'Yes, Neethu. What is it?' he asked, his voice annoyed.

She spoke with slight hesitation 'Andrew...' Her eyes went wide and twinkled. He showed his palm in denial.

'You can call me doctor,' he snapped. Her wide lips aligned to a horizontal line in upset.

‘Okay, Doctor. I want to talk to you.’ She bit her nails while waiting for his answer. Andrew slightly inclined his head towards her, narrowing his eyes in an attempt to listen. ‘Are you..’ She sighed. ‘Are you married? ’ she finally asked, grinding her palms against each other.

‘No, why do you ask?’

‘Really! I hope you don’t have a girlfriend yet.’ She could not resist the grin on her face.

‘I think this conversation is beyond your professional needs. Do you mind refraining?’

‘I agree, it’s a personal question. But I just want to be honest with you about my thoughts and intentions. This has been on my mind since you arrived. I really like you.’

Andrew frowned without meaning to. ‘Listen, thank you for being honest. I don’t want this to repeat again. I am strictly not encouraging this. You’re at work. I expect you to do just that. You might get fired if this repeats. Clear?’

‘Yes. Can we talk about this later?’ she asked, pleased.

‘No, Neethu. Now go to work.’ He pointed at the entrance.

‘Okay, and... the patient is not taking her tablets. Her food intake is only once a day. I tried telling her multiple times. Also, there is no use taking tablets without food. So...’

'I don't want you to force her anyway. I will take care of it. You can leave it to me.'

'But the chief doctor said no course should be missed.'

'I can talk to him. Shouldn't be your problem.'

'Okay.' Neethu instantly walked away with her lips tight.

Samantha listened to the whole conversation which reminded her of the only experience she had with love, being a messenger for Simon and Preethi. She noticed that the nurse resembled Preethi from her childhood, fair, fit, with much radiant skin and pretty. Samantha had been the adorable kid from the primary when Simon and Preethi were studying higher secondary. She admired the way Preethi looked. She used to pass love letters between them. Samantha was not only the carrier of the letters but also the subject most of the time. She used to deliver and pick up letters at the play area or the restroom. She loved the bond between the three of them, though she never knew what relationship Simon and Preethi held. 'You should never tell Mum about Preethi. She is our secret friend. Okay?' Simon used to bid his sister. She wanted to relive those precious days.

'Sorry, just ignore that. This usually doesn't happen,' Andrew said with his tone sunk in embarrassment, his face almost red.

'Can you call home?' Samantha interrupted.

Andrew gasped, not expecting a call request from her.

'Well... ' He rubbed his palms together, baffled. He could not reach her eyes which were longing for a positive answer. 'Look, it's already half past seven and your parents might panic if we call them at this time. Let's—'

'I want to talk to Simon!' Her voice was firm with certainty. Andrew had not, even in his dreams, expected that he would be in this situation. 'Well, let's… let's do one thing. Let's call tomorrow. Okay?'

Samantha couldn't insist much more and turned back to continue gazing at the sea.

CHAPTER 6

Andrew left the dorm abruptly to avoid any further requests from Samantha that he could not fulfill even if he wished to. His words were implanted into Samantha's head firmly. She practiced sentences to express her feelings and questions to ask multiple times in her head. The idea of talking to her brother the next morning made her feel lighter. She smiled to her own surprise, but the smile vanished at once listening to footsteps approach.

A hollow ceramic plate filled with three rice cakes soaked in lentil soup was placed on the wooden table. 'Please have your dinner. I'll get your tablets after that.' Neethu spoke a bit assertively and went back to the waiting room. Samantha's shrunken eyes were constant elsewhere but on Neethu, until she left the room. She admired her attire though she hated her tone. Neethu had pitch-black hair tied in a bun, radiant skin, and the pleats of her skirt fell perfectly across the curve her lower body made. Samantha looked down at herself with a loathsome look and searched for a mirror around her. She found a wardrobe with a long mirror along its length. This was the first time she actually took a good look at the entire room.

She dragged herself with tiny steps to stand in front of the mirror. She gasped, narrowing her eyes, clearly saddened at the sight of herself. She was nothing like how she remembered to be, a subtle, innocent girl living a joyful life amongst the compact circle of family and friends. Her eyes slowly captured the background the mirror reflected; the surroundings of white walls, a bed with a grey comforter, and a wall-hanging lamp, each and every object gave her a headshot of the reality of not being home. She stood as close as she could to the wardrobe, the tip of her nose almost touching the mirror. Her pupils narrowed. Her eyes shuffled from the left to the right. She blinked a couple of times, making sure her eyes were the same as she saw back when she used to get ready for school. Her eyelids were dry and wrinkly. She remembered how her friends used to admire the beauty of her slightly brown eyes. The puffiness under the eyes bore a purplish shadow. She reached her forehead upon noticing a scar, she brushed it delicately with her left arm, tilting her chin to the right. Her eyes were drawn to the white gauze that wrapped her forearm since the first day. She tussled with the bandage and removed it within a minute only to reveal the worst scar on her left forearm. She stepped back a bit in shock from her own reflection. She ground her teeth in disgust looking at the one-inch wide scar on the forearm, almost close to the wrist. She tried to touch it but the edges still hurt. She noticed that even her fingers bore scars in the space between the pointing and the middle fingers which seemed to wear multiple bruises.

She looked at her rangy body next. She pressed her palm against the hollow arch made of ribs and slowly upwards. She noticed her breasts generously developed, they weren't the same size from her latest memory. Her shoulder bone was evident, making room for almost a fistful of sand, it was touched by the tips of her hair that were brittle and longer than usual. The radiant, flawless skin she once had was now lifeless. She sat right in front of the mirror and sobbed, reflecting the hideous appearance. She sobbed for whatever happened to her, for not having an idea of what she had endured. She wondered what situations could have pushed her to this moment. Samantha again felt a twister in her head, pulling her eyes and breathing inwards to the back of her head. She wrestled with herself on the floor pulling her hair tight. She made low-based noises that sounded like a dog growling. A nurse rushed into the room listening to the loud noises late in the night.

'Samantha. What? What is happening?' She held Samantha's hands with much effort to protect her from pulling her own hair. The nurse reached for her phone from the front pocket and dialed Andrew asking for rescue. 'Give her Risperidone. I'll be there in five minutes.'

'Please come soon doctor,' she pleaded.

Samantha was calmed down from a dreadful situation with the help of the injection. Andrew reached the dorm within a few minutes as promised. He cringed upon the heart-rending sight of the person he was completely responsible for. He checked her pulse, carried her, who was unconscious and curled up on the floor, with both his arms, and gently placed her on the bed. He stayed up in the waiting room the whole night to make sure he was there should the situation occur again.

CHAPTER 7

The breeze wafted away Samantha's thoughts. The rhythm of the waves shut her existence from the exterior world. She sat by the shore caught by the horizon. The sky looked like it was draped with an orange gradient saree. The sea seemed to refine her soul with every hit of a wave. She observed the kids making sand castles, some were challenging the water, and they'd go closer to the shore when the sea was taken back and run as fast as possible when the waves came back. It occurred to her that she had already been to Chennai for one of their summer vacations. The memories bloomed fresh in her mind where she along with her brother used to play hide and seek at the back of random people, and how their mother ripped both of them for doing that. "What if someone took you guys?" she'd always asked.

Samantha smirked. Andrew sat next to her in silence for a long time. 'It's beautiful, isn't it?' he asked with a subtle voice. She nodded without looking away from the sea. 'Do you want anything to eat?' He pointed at the fire-crackling corn and ice cream vehicles. She shook her head in response 'Okay. Well, listen, I wanna talk to you about something.' Samantha frowned. 'Kind of important,' he finished in a whisper.

'Sure.' She turned her torso slightly toward Andrew.

'Well, how do I put it? Okay, lemme ask you a few questions first.' He took a deep breath before he started. 'What is your full name?'

She stared, knowing it was such a silly question to ask at this point. 'Samantha.'

'Your full name?'

'Samantha Sebastian.'

'Good! And your age?' She blinked before answering 'Seventeen...'

'Your parents are?'

'Victor Sebastian and Layla Sebastian.'

'Great. Now, can you tell me what is your latest memory? What do you remember being the last thing that happened before you came here?'

Samantha took several minutes to think and could not come up with an answer. 'Tell me whatever comes to your mind, will you?'

She closed her eyes, forcing herself hard to match anything she remembers to her current self. 'I only remember Bunny's words. My brother. That was after my twelfth-grade results were issued, not immediately, guess a few days later. I had cleared my board exams in the first class. Since my dad was a bank manager he always wanted either Bunny or myself to become his legacy. But Bunny was interested in buildings and their designs. He graduated in architecture as he wished. While my dad was persuading me to get into accounts, I asked Bunny to decide for me. He said "This is the time when you can decide what you wanna be in the future. Do you see yourself at a desk making your life monotonous?" He said, "Everyone has their own dreams. It is not necessary that one should follow their parents' path. Who will live your dream if you spend your life fulfilling your parents'? Are you gonna burden your children just like them? Listen to your heart, Samantha. I have heard you talking about what you really wanna do. And that's very rare. I want you to realize that and become that person. Parents are only the pillars of your building. *You* have to decide how to build it and what it should look like. Your career is in your hands. Acknowledge it and rule it." He is a very practical person,' she said, gazing at Andrew.

'Yeah, I can tell.' Andrew was honestly impressed by the incident she described, but also regretted that it might trigger more memories of Simon.

'I miss him. He wouldn't leave me alone like this, it's only this time. He should be busy,' she proudly said, narrowing her eyes. It only then rang a bell to him, letting alone the memory loss. She still doesn't know the truth about Simon.

'See, you… you might currently be in a situation where you forget a little bit of your past.' he slowly said.

'What? No, I don't think I'm forgetting anything.'

'You are sam. You have a loss of memory.'

She froze for several moments looking at Andrew.

'Yes. And you're not seventeen. You're twenty-two now.' Samantha almost skipped a beat. She kept looking at him without a blink, her mouth wide open.

And…Simon is no more, he wanted to say. *I have started the mess, I might as well finish it by telling her everything at once.* But he refrained due to him being skeptical about her comeback, and most importantly about handling her in the middle of the seashore.

Is this similar to something I saw in movies? She had no words to utter. She heard Andrew's words on a loop. The beach waves could not prevail over the sound of her heart pounding. She tried to connect the dots, waking up in an unknown place, looking quite different from what she remembered, with all the scars she discovered on her body and most importantly not having an idea of her last memory. All this added to the fact that she had lost her memory. 'How?' she finally asked after several minutes.

'Where do I start?' He scratched his forehead with his pointer finger. 'Well, I told you about the other day—' He abruptly stopped from spilling another word of her past to her. She frowned as whatever he said didn't make any sense. 'Well... it was an accident.'

'Does that mean all those memory loss stories in the movies are true?' she asked with a mystery on her face.

'Well, I believe movies are only recreation of real stories. You know what I mean?' he said, squinting his eyes. She felt silly about skipping a few years in memory. Her eyes were dragged to the shoreline unintendedly, She noticed the large waves erase the traces of grey shoreline made by the small wave and smirked at it. *Nothing is permanent.* She had wondered how her life would've been all those years. What kind of a person was I? Definitely kind. I've always been kind. And inquisitive of course. Oh, I would've gone to college, had friends and all. She smiled looking at the sky. I wonder if I had a great time in college. I hope I've gotten wiser. What future I had made. Ha! Now I understand why I am with a psychiatrist. Her eyes shone only for a moment and dimmed the moment she remembered the scars on her body. The rambling thoughts about her memory loss were overtaken by thinking about the situations that would've led to those scars.

'Nothing to worry. I have seen quite a few lose their memory due to various reasons. This can be cured by following a set of procedures. I'll take care of that, Sam. You just have to trust us. You know what I mean?' Though Andrew's words bore assurance and confidence, he had a battle of thoughts in his head about whether or not to unveil the loss of her brother. He also worried that the news might drive her back to the hell she was previously in. Looking at Samantha's profile glow in the last golden ray of sunlight, he pledged to himself that she would be his responsibility and that it was in his hands to make her a path to new life.

Andrew had exhibited confidence only with Samantha. The act of having to talk to her parents gave him chills from the inside. He gathered all his courage together and dialed Layla.

Layla jerked to the known ringtone of her phone. She was pulled back from the virtual world she was dwelling in by looking at the wall full of pictures filled with her son and daughter.

'Please don't give me bad news.'

'Not at all.'

'Tell me, Andrew. I hope Sam is okay.'

'She is absolutely fine, Ma'am. In fact, I told her about the memory loss today.'

Layla gasped. 'What…then what happened?'

'She was okay with it. Did not react much, really.'

'I can't believe this.'

'I know.' He smiled excitedly.

'I think I can come over then. I can take care of her. What do you say?'

'Well, Ma'am, it is a bit of a risk. You see, now she is eating well, meditating in the mornings. She takes her tablets on time and doesn't have tantrums. But, if she gets exposed to her past events or persons, or even places for that matter, there is a threat she might get flashed with the past. And I'm afraid that could take her back again. You know what I mean?'

'But, still, I think I should be there. I can check on her each and every minute.'

'Ma'am, trust me. Neethu is here to take care of Samantha. I am here. Everything is going to be okay. Things are going as expected and we don't want any factor that triggers her past until she tops her health.'

'Are you saying that this memory loss is for good?'

'Maybe.'

'But, she has to remember eventually, and she will, won't she?'

'She definitely will. I'm quite positive about that. I just feel this is too early. If you don't give her enough time to heal, there is more of a chance for her to return to her past life.'

CHAPTER 8

Samantha had been twisting the Rubik's cube randomly since the previous night. She could not sleep, being unable to settle her mind. Thoughts about her past were spreading like wildfire. She slowly started to feel traumatized from the inside. This time, she pretty much knew what was going to happen. She clenched her jaw, closed her eyelids tight, and kept herself prepared. She saw herself and Simon as kids.

Her young, curious eyes were ready to learn everything they came across, and his innocent laughter made people surrender themselves. They were playing, running with joy all around the backyard fenced with old coconut trees, lemon trees, neem trees, and many random plants behind their house. The soothing evening sun rays cast onto their faces, through the small gaps left between the branches. Simon hid at the back of a coconut tree, his forehead leaning against the tree while he covered the sides of his eyes with his palms.

"Ten, nine, eight..." He started counting in reverse. Meanwhile, Samantha ran into their house to hide. Simon had heard the noise she made while running across the bed of dried leaves that were spread all over the ground. He went straight into the bedroom, as hiding under the cot was Samantha's first and favorite spot inside the house every time they played hide and seek.

'Ahh, I found you!' Simon screamed, pointing at Samantha while she simultaneously screamed, 'No!'

'Now it's your turn!' Samantha said innocently, jumping on her toes.

'I know, and I bet you cannot catch me whatsoever.' Simon knew that the only words Samantha went crazy about were 'I bet', and he said them to make his game more challenging. Simon slowly sneaked out of the lawn through the back gate as Samantha counted her numbers. Going out of the lawn was one thing both Simon and Samantha were forbidden to do when they visited their grandparents' house.

Samantha searched the whole house and found the back gate open. She thought of informing her mother immediately but the challenge pulled her back. She did not want to lose to her brother. She sneaked out swiftly towards the vast greenery filled with various kinds of trees, which almost looked like a jungle. Samantha moved forward between the thick trees calling out 'Bunny' as loud as possible. She heard birds flutter and the branches move in various directions and could not decide on which direction Simon could've gone. She turned around, not able to figure out the path she came from.

She saw a light brown insect moving next to her right foot which could not have been differentiated from a dried leaf if not given attention. Samantha caught her breath wondering what more could be creeping around her with nature's skin. She heard a noise behind her and her heart almost seized. Her eyes widened when she turned her head. 'Bunny!' she ran towards him and held his hand to feel secure.

'Shh!' Simon gestured to her to be quiet. Simon walked with tiny steps avoiding much noise, Samantha followed him the same way.

'I saw a baby snake,' Simon whispered.

'What are you saying?' She stopped and refused to walk any further.

'It should be near that pond, let's catch it.'

'No. Why do you want to catch it?' Samantha unclenched her palm from Simon's.

'It will come into our house. I'm sure you do not want that to happen.'

'No! But I also don't want to catch a snake.'

'A baby snake!'

'Whatever!'

'Okay, you go home. I'll go alone,' said Simon and ran beyond their house.

Samantha stared at their house in a dilemma; she wanted to escape from this place, but she also wanted Simon not to hurt that snake. Now that she knew she was safe and where her home was, Samantha wanted the baby snake to feel the same. She ran into the woods following the path Simon had taken. It was later in the day and the sky was almost purplish. She kept calling Simon as she moved faster. Within a blink, a hard wind hit Samantha's face. Her steps felt multiple times heavier due to the thick sand under her feet. She was baffled by being literally deserted in a moment. She was not surrounded by the forest anymore. A humongous snake crept through the sand and reached her.

'Sam, RUN!' Simon appeared from nowhere. The snake elevated itself beyond the clouds within seconds, leaving the rest of its body in a four-layered swirl on the sand. Samantha and Simon stood there looking at the snake, awestruck. The snake came back down with its mouth opened wide, the force of its descent made the place a sandstorm. Simon shoved her away, while the snake gobbled him up.

Samantha slowly opened her moist and bloodshot eyes. She found herself panting, drenched in sweat. Everything she saw before the sand storm was true; they had bet for the chocolate goodies their grandfather offered after hide-and-seek. Though everything after the sand storm was absurd. She made herself sit on the bed throwing her head in her hands.

Why is it always Bunny? Bunny... Bunny. I need to talk to you. She walked up and down the bedroom in hurry.

'Hi, how is Sam?' She heard Andrew's voice; he had gotten there at the usual time as he always did.

'I think she is sleeping,' Neethu said.

Samantha rushed to him as soon as she heard his voice, with bloodshot eyes and wet clothes. 'Andrew! I need to talk to Simon. Please, take me home, please.' Samantha pleaded with a broken voice.

'What, what's wrong?' Andrew held Samantha by her shoulders.

'I want to see my brother,' she insisted.

Andrew initially doubted if Samantha got her memories back, then it occurred to him that if so, she would not be asking for Simon now. 'Wait, wait.' Andrew jolted her. 'Tell me what happened first, then I'll call your home. What happened?' She explained to Andrew the nightmares she had been getting. Her breath was erratic while she spoke; she took regular pauses and gave all the details. This time she believed that Andrew would help in getting her closer to her brother, while Andrew also heartfully wished that he could do the same. After patiently listening to Samantha's nightmares, he said, 'Easy. Easy Sam. It's not at all good for you to panic like this. Please, calm down. This might only be a coincidence.'

'This can in no way be a coincidence. Andrew, I think Bunny is in some danger. I have to warn him about this. Please help me talk to him. Please.' Samantha's red-veined eyes dilated.

'Gosh…' Andrew did not know how to manage her instincts. 'No. Sam, calm down. He is fine. You need not worry. It's absolutely normal for you to get these thoughts. But leave it at that. Please.'

'No, it is not normal. It's alarming. I have to talk to him. It's important.' She held both his arms tight and looked straight into his eyes. 'Please understand. This has happened before. I had nightmares about my cat a week before I lost her,' she said. She held his rolled sleeve tighter with her wet palms. 'Please!'.

Andrew swallowed, being dumbstruck listening to her experience of instincts. N*ow how in the world would I tell her the truth?* he fretted. He held her hand which was pressing tightly on his sleeve and spoke softly. 'I think you're just spoiling your peace of mind by comparing random things.'

'Oh, no.' She pushed him away and yelled with rage, 'No, no, no, no…' She banged the wall with both her hands, her eyes bulged out. 'Why are you not understanding? I don't know what the problem is here. I am asking for my brother, not a random person. I am not asking you to take me there, just one call. Why are you guys doing this to me? I feel like I'm in jail.' She broke down, dropping herself on the floor.

Andrew felt that he was the reason for Samantha being pushed to that situation. *Had I told her the truth along with the memory loss, she would not have to handle this now. Or would I be handling it worse?* He felt blue looking at Samantha's condition. 'Neethu, take her inside. I'll be back.' He walked out of the room having no other option.

'Doctor. Andrew, wait.' He heard a dense voice of an old man while he was rushing up the staircase. The chief doctor walked towards the stairs near Samantha's dorm entrance.

'Hello, doctor,' Andrew wished hesitantly.

'Can I talk to you for a minute?'

'Yeah, sure.' Andrew climbed back and accompanied the chief doctor while they spoke. The two walked across the long corridor while they conversed.

'How are things with the patient from room 25? I heard it's tough. Is that true?'

'No. No, Doctor. Tough is a big word and it is totally irrelevant. I don't know who...'

The chief doctor showed his palm, interrupting Andrew. 'I don't care if the patient is tough or not, all I need is progress. I hope you're aware of the patient from Kerala. His condition was very critical and no one informed me about it. You know what happened, at last, right?'

Samantha walked out of her room searching for Andrew and was stalled by the sight of the doctors conversing.

'Look, I'm responsible for anything that happens here,' the chief doctor continued. 'I don't want stubborn patients; I can change them to a different doctor if you cannot handle them or change the hospital that will give them the perfect treatment and inform their parents after that. I don't want to listen to stories of stubbornness anymore. Okay? If you're unable to manage tantrums, just quit. Don't wait until the last moment when they would run away somewhere. If anything at all happens, Andrew, you will report to me. Alright?'

'I assure you, Doctor, nothing of that sort will happen. I will make sure everything's fine.'

'Good for you.' The chief doctor promptly left the hallway.

Andrew climbed up the stairs straight to the terrace. His face and body were expelling fumes of irritation and failure. He counted from ten in reverse and took long breaths, his eyes fixed on a pigeon beside him which was moving her head front and back, rolling her eyes as she walked. He took a few minutes to consciously indulge in the tiny act of art by the pigeon. A cheer travelled from inside to his lips and to his eyes. The state of relief did not last long before the idea of telling Samantha the truth popped into his head. Amongst the various patients he had dealt with, Andrew had never taken their situations personally, for that was what he'd been taught. Doctors need to be empathetic and not sympathetic to their patients. He knew that Samantha was not just a patient to him. After all, that was the reason he followed her to a different city. He recalled and reminded himself of the moment when he first saw her. How she reminded him of his mother. He held his palms, one in another, tight and kept them close to his heart, facing the sky. *Maa,* he thought, *Please help me help her. I love you.*

He descended the staircase back to Samantha deciding to unveil the truth which is haunting her indirectly. By the time he got back to the dorm, he was struck by a surprise. Samantha was taking her tablets with the help of Neethu. She had witnessed the whole conversation between Andrew and the chief doctor and thought it was unfair for him to be penalized by his chief because of her. And that he was only trying to help her.

CHAPTER 9

Neethu stood around five feet apart from the staircase that led to the topmost terrace. She wore a sweater on top of the nurse uniform and tucked her hands into the front pockets. The beach waves seemed to scream continuously across the quiet roads, conveying a message to the city which was prepared to go to bed.

'Shall I get your jerkin? It's cold,' Neethu asked politely.

'No, thank you. This feels calm inside.' Samantha stared at the sea in the quietness.

'Thank you for taking tablets today. I really appreciate it. I mean, I know how intense the situation was.'

Samantha gave the slightest smile in response. 'But Andrew… sorry, the doctor never wanted to force it on you.'

'It's okay. You can call him that when you're talking to me. I know you like him. I heard your conversation the other day.'

'Gosh. I was so stupid. Sorry about that.'

'C'mon, did you get to talk to him after that?'

'Oh! Don't even ask. He keeps escaping whenever I catch him alone.' They both laughed under the dim light, their voices echoing against the noise of beach waves. Neethu's phone rang; she drew it from the front pocket making the subtle ringtone go louder. 'Wow. Hundred years.' Her face glowed in the light emitted from the screen. 'Hello, Doctor. No, we're on the terrace. Samantha wanted to get some air.'

'Hi,' Neethu said as Andrew climbed the stairs two at a time.

'All okay?' he calmly asked, catching a breath.

'Yes, Doctor. Just getting some air.'

'Cool.' He gave himself a tour across the concrete fence to make sure no other person was loitering around. 'Wow, It's getting cold, isn't it? I think it's better to get back down. What do you think?' Andrew looked to Samantha who sat in the dark, on the staircase that led to the topmost terrace. She did not respond.

'Hey. I'm so sorry, Sam.' He spoke in a tone lower than usual. 'About this morning. I could not help you. But I can explain.'

'No. I should be sorry.' Her voice was calm but sharp. 'This is my fault. I know, I am all flawed. I don't even have an idea how worried my family would be to have me treated far from them for memory loss, or something I'm not even aware of. It must be costing them a lot. And on top of it, I'm troubling you all.'

Andrew took a minute to figure out where Samantha was getting to. 'Sam…'

'I'm sorry.' She rose from the staircase and stood facing Andrew. 'I can behave as expected.' She continued to talk, 'I can wake up early in the morning with no nightmares; I can meditate with no deviations; I can chug in meal after meal and medicines after medicines like an eating machine. I will not ask to talk to my family anymore. I can also change my skin if only it was possible and look absolutely like a normal person. I can be a good person or a good patient, just as you wish.' She took deep breaths.

'Did you… did you by any chance listen to the chief doctor's words?' He frowned.

'I did.'

'Oh, damn. Listen, that has nothing to do with you. In fact, he was not talking about you. Okay? You need not be a perfect patient. And if you ask me about being a perfect person, there is no one as such. Everything you said now will happen, but the chief doctor… or I, or even you should give it some time.' Andrew threw his hands in the air. He sighed and said, 'I want to tell you one thing, but before that, you have to make a promise.'

'Andrew, I don't think I'm ready to listen to any—'

'It's important, I insist,' he interrupted.

'What?'

'Promise?'

'What promise?'

'Well, your journey here is very important. To you, your family, and also to me. So, whatever I tell you now should not affect your journey here. Precisely, you should be here until this treatment is completed and you should not think otherwise. Okay?'

'I think I have heard the most unexpected thing, about my memory loss. What could be worse than that...'

'Well, that is what life is. You can imagine how perfect it could be, but not how worse it could get.' She sharply looked at him, listening carefully. 'We did not want to reveal this to you until the treatment was completed, but things don't seem to be getting any better. I believe you will be strong and cope with what I am going to tell you.'

Samantha took a deep breath, looking at the stars.

'Your family is now smaller than you remember.'

'What do you mean?'

'We lost your–'

She jerked away from Andrew with her eyes widening. She shoved her fingers into her ears, blocking any more of his words to enter. She shook her head forcefully, spilling out the tears that already filled her eyes.

WHAT!! What the heck was he going to tell? I don't. I don't want to believe this. I don't want to listen. I don't want this to happen. No. No. No. No. No. No. Words burst into her head.

She kept saying, 'no' multiple times, shaking her head vigorously. The conversation made Samantha's blood pressure erratic, and she fell unconscious. Andrew was filled with guilt for deciding to reveal the truth to her despite the chief doctor's opposition.

The next morning, Samantha woke up to find Neethu and Andrew staring at her. She remembered the conversation from last night but did not know how it ended.

'Sorry.' She twined her fingers together.

'What? I don't see why?' Andrew said.

'I know that I reacted inappropriately. I think...' She kept looking at her fingers.

'Not really, don't worry about it.'

'Is it true? What you told me last night?' she asked, looking sharply at Andrew's eyes.

He stayed quiet.

'I spoke to mom recently... it can't be her.' Her voice broke.

'It's not her.' He shook his head.

Her eyes widened. 'Da-daddy…' She dragged out the word in hesitation, while her heart raced. Andrew slowly shook his head again. Samantha was petrified to an extent where she felt her joints jarred, her bloodstream frozen and she could not even blink. All the moments with Simon ran in front of her. Starting with the little games he played with her while he babysat, the lessons when he taught her to improve her grades, and the constant care he gave when she was affected by chicken pox; he never left her alone but amused her with various skits just to make her smile. The time he came to school to check and feed her during recess while all his friends would head to the playground after lunch. The courage he showed to stand up for her while she was bullied in school. The guidance he gave in each and every decision she made. He had been a backbone to his sister and whenever she faced a hurdle in life, she would turn to him first.

Andrew called her thrice before she responded. 'I can understand how you feel and how close you were to your brother...'

'Origin,' she said, 'he was my origin! More than a mother to me.' The nerves on her neck tightened, and her lips shivered uncontrollably. She dug her nails into the back of her head. She wanted to run toward a speeding vehicle, jump off from the tallest building, get lost in the middle of the sea, or get crushed to deep inside the hell out of devastation.

'Sam,' Andrew called louder this time. 'I'm sorry for your loss.' He sat next to her holding her hand.

'Loss,' she repeated. Samantha had heard the phrase "sorry for the loss" several times since her childhood. But it was only at that very moment did she know what it meant. She realized she had lost his presence; that she had lost the joy of calling his name; that she had lost feeling his vibe; that she had lost all the conversations she would have made with him in the future; that she lost being captured by his gaze; that she had lost all the moments she would get surrounded by his arms; that she had lost the most valuable guidance he would've given from his own experience; that she had lost hearing him crack a joke; that she had lost laughing with him and getting scolded for her mischief; that she had lost betting on random things like they always did. That she had lost learning what was right and what was wrong from his conscience. That she had lost the part of the family he would've made. That she had lost her favorite person in this world, and that she had lost her origin itself.

The reality finally hit her after several minutes of rapid activity mentally while staying still physically. She swallowed a tide of emotion from overflowing. Her eyes were red and her throat choked. She ran into the restroom and locked the door behind her. She sobbed loudly in the little privacy available and did not care about the voices asking her to open the door.

CHAPTER 10

Her steps weighed more than she could bear. She struggled to catch up with Andrew's pace, though his walk was snail-like. 'Do you want to sit here?' He pointed at a bench near the shore.

Samantha nodded. She had spent two whole days within those four walls before she could take a step out. Crying, cursing the gods for taking her only brother and giving her a condition that vanished all her latest memories with him. She spoke to her parents and learned how this had happened. 'It's unfortunate, Simon had an accident,' they said. It took a great effort from Andrew to make Samantha step out of the dorm which she thought was her territory to dive into the misery and bury herself.

'Hey... look.' He pointed at a tiny crab crawling sideways towards the sea, while they both sat on the bench facing the shore. Samantha looked at the crab without moving a single muscle on her face.

Andrew sighed. 'You guys were really close, weren't you?' he asked calmly. The talk of Simon rushed her face with blood, turning her cheeks and nose almost pink. Her eyes teared within a fleeting moment. She stretched her neck backward just for a minute, closing her eyes and breathing hard before she looked at Andrew and said, 'We weren't just siblings, he was more than a brother to me,' she said softly, rubbing her tears.

'I... I still can't believe this. As far as I remember, he was young, energetic, inspiring, responsible, and of course, short-tempered. He was a short-tempered person. Still, to think that I cannot see him anymore is just, it is killing me inside.' She broke down.

'I understand.'

'He didn't deserve to leave. He had great dreams to achieve in architecture. Why did God take him, Andrew? He should've taken me instead. He should've taken all my years to heal him. Why him?'

She looked at Andrew with her wet eyes and frowned as if expecting a justification.

'You know, Sam... one day, a woman lost her young son, just a few days after her husband had died. Her son was her only hope and she was devastated by the loss. A few of her well-wishers suggested she approached Buddha. "He is really compassionate and may help revive your child," they said.

'The woman rushed over with the body of the child. Buddha looked at the woman, told her to put the child in front of him, and said "Yes, I will revive your child. But you will have to fulfil one condition." The woman said that she was ready to fulfil any condition Buddha gave. Buddha said, "It is a simple condition. I never make big requirements from people." He asked her to go to the town and bring some mustard seeds, but the condition was that they could be only from a family in which no one had ever died.'

'Why?' Samantha interrupted, unmindfully.

Andrew continued narrating, 'The woman also could not see the point in Buddha's requirement. But she rushed with great hope; she knew that every house in that town had mustard seeds, as that was the only crop the people grew. She knocked on each and every door and stated the requirement. People were ready to give her cartloads of mustard seeds, but she couldn't find a single house without people dying. "Many people have died in our house," they would say. When the night dawned, the woman came to her senses and realized that she had knocked on every door in that village but could not find a house without death. She then knew that death was inevitable. That it happens to everybody, and there will be no one who does not experience the pain of grief.' Samantha froze, she stared at the ground, lost in thoughts.

'Are you okay?' Andrew asked to which she nodded back.

'So, she went back to Buddha a different person,' he continued. 'The child was lying there and Buddha was waiting. "Where are the mustard seeds?" he asked. The woman fell to his feet and cried, "I understand, Buddha. Today my son died, a few days before my husband died, and in the future, I will also die. Now, I don't want to retrieve my son from death," she said. Buddha said that that was the purpose of sending her. So that she could be awakened. "See eternal life. Don't let the human form blind your connection with the soul. Your relationship with your family is an eternal one and it is unbreakable by any force"," he said.'

Andrew tried to look into her eyes to reach her soul. 'This might sound pointless to you now. But remember that everyone has to… remind themselves of this story whenever they get the question of 'why?' I'm not saying that you should forget about the person and continue with your life. Understand that this is the natural cycle, that wherever there is life, there will be death. Hey, lemme ask you something. Do you like Mother Teresa?'

She looked puzzled and answered, 'Yes,' nodding her head.

'Exactly. She doesn't belong to your family. You haven't met her. You wouldn't have even seen her, but you like her. How? It's the remembrance. Remembrance connects to memories, memories connecting the activities she did as a person. That is what is keeping her alive among us, not her physical presence. Yes, if we love someone, we love unconditionally, don't limit that to only when they are alive. Just practice loving them equally even otherwise. All we can do is cherish their memories. You know what I mean...'

They both allowed some silence to fill in while she processed everything in her head. 'I'll wait by the car. You take your time.' He walked past her, hoping she'd give his words a thought.

She took around thirty minutes of solitude to cry out her sorrow. She wept when no one was around, rubbed her tears when people passed, and wept again. A deep sigh ended the loop. Her eyes felt lighter and her vision got clearer. She sat with her spine bent and shoulders curled forward, her glance shuffled left and right with jerks before she looked at the sky and said, 'I love you, Bunny. A part of my heart will always be with you!'

Samantha got back to the car when she felt a bit light at heart. They were both comfortable in their silence; it wasn't awkward anymore. They had reached the dorm before she could decide on how to thank him.

'Okay. Good night then. Take care. I'll see you tomorrow.' He waved while she got out of the car.

She peered at him through the window. *Thank you so much. I feel better now*, her heart wanted to say. 'Good night!' her brain prompted.

CHAPTER 11

BANGALORE

6 months before

Samantha's hands and legs trembled. She tried multiple times to step into Simon's room; she'd climb up a couple of stairs and rush back to her room. It was only after a few weeks that she was able to enter the place Simon had spent most of his time. She entered with trembling steps. Every corner of the room flooded her with memories. She touched and felt every little thing in the room, like a piece of art in an exhibition. She ran her hands through his wardrobe, picked up his favorite dark green shirt, and held it close to her heart. She recalled the first time he had worn the shirt on his birthday. 'You looked handsome in this shirt, Bunny,' she whispered.

She needed no water source for her tears, they were emerging from a broken heart. 'I don't want to forget a single thing about you! The way you speak, your gait, your smile, the way you set the silky straight strands falling on your forehead, the way you eat...' She fretted. She took a deep breath gradually and sighed. The reek of cigarettes in the room slowly pushed her to a nostalgic space from her childhood at once.

She remembered something they had done every summer when they were schooling. Bunny and her would raise a bet on who finished their share of watermelon first. She smiled; it was not just a random nickname. That was how he looked with his two prominent front teeth, like a bunny. Which turned out to be handsome as he grew up. She smiled at the shirt she had in her hand.

Being six years younger than him, she knew he took advantage of how much smaller she was. Whilst she was literally feeling breathless with her mouth stuffed with watermelon, in contrast, Bunny seemed to be doing it effortlessly. The stake for this is to watch their favorite channel in the allotted one hour of television time in the evening. She was sure it would end up on some random sports channel he would binge.

It took a while for Samantha to realize that she was alone, the memory fading away. Her parents tried hard to make conversations with her the rest of the day. Eventually, she spoke less, slept less, ate less, and thought more, only with Simon in her head. She visited every nook and corner of the room. She felt the impression of all the paperwork Simon had worked on and thought about the strain he would've gone through in order to get those details done. She touched the blunt tips of the pencils he used. *These would have gone through a great deal of struggle*, she thought, looking at the course surface of the pencil lead. She spent the rest of the day picturing him in his clothes one by one.

The next day she visited the room feeling disappointed as there was no smell of remembrance. The smell of cigarettes. She missed her brother more without it. She recalled seeing a pack of cigarettes somewhere in the room which she failed to recollect. Samantha searched for the box everywhere she could reach in the room, in the drawer of the bedside table, in his cupboard, in the rack that is attached to the TV table, in his bag, and in the toiletry shelf. She was astonished at how a familiar smell could recall a person's presence; and she was devastated, not being able to feel it again. She thought she had found a final resort that gave her the precious feeling of Simon's presence. She doubted if her mother might have dumped it away in the garbage.

Samantha remembered that Simon always used to keep his cigarette boxes on top of his wooden wardrobe. She rushed to the wardrobe hoping to find it there. She climbed the stool and was saddened by the empty space. She fell down on her knees right there. A teardrop rolled onto her cheek without a moment's delay. Her eyes rolled everywhere in a brief thought. She could remember the golden pack with creepy photographs on it. She closed her eyes and thought for a second. Glimpses appeared from her photographic memory. She walked straight to the cot, lifted up the mattress on one corner, and repeated the same on the other three corners. She had finally found a pack at the last corner, under the mattress.

She grabbed the box and held it close to her with a sigh. She quickly closed the door of the room before her mother or father could come. She wanted to light a cigarette but only realized later that she did not have a fire source. She definitely knew that there would be a matchbox on the altar. She shoved the cigarette pack in the elastic waist of her pyjamas. She sneaked into the living room and got the matchbox in no time. She got back to Simon's room and was all ready to light a cigarette. She took a cigarette from the pack with trembling hands and held it straight. She initially struggled with lighting a matchstick with the cigarette in another hand. She kept the cigarette down and lit a matchstick first, she held the bud of the cigarette and lit the other end before the fire was gone. She had fired half of the cigarette and dropped it down. The cigarette was burnt all over the paper wrap inappropriately. Samantha knew that was not how cigarettes were lit but she was happy she at least could smell the disgusting cigarette smoke. She wondered how Simon could've taken this into his lungs. She remembered the day when Simon had first smoked and confessed to her.

'Dude, why is your mouth stinking? What did you eat?' she yelled, blocking her breath with both hands.

'Shh! Don't shout. I smoked and I wanted to share this moment with someone. You are the only person with whom I can share this now.'

'Are you crazy! Wait, I'm gonna tell this to Mumma.'

'Hey... Sammy Sammy. Please! Please shut your mouth. Else I'm not gonna share anything with you ever again. You'll not be my secret fairy. If that is fine, then go, go tell Mumma. I'm okay to get kicked out of the house.' Samantha looked at him briefly for a moment. 'Will you share all your secrets with me?'

'Of course, my pumpkin, who else I'll share with?'

'Okay. I won't tell Mumma.'

The door was knocked on twice, throwing her out of the memory bubble.

'Sam!' Layla screamed from the other side of the door. The cigarette was almost burnt and the whole room reeked of burnt bud when Samantha got back from her nostalgic moment.

'Haan, Ma.' She was startled by the arrival of her mother.

'What are you doing? Open the door.' Since Simon was gone, Samantha was keenly observed by her parents. They had already noticed her being isolated most of the time. Samantha was still dealing with the cigarette mess when her mother asked her to open the door for the third time.

'Nothing, Ma, everything is alright.'

'Okay, then open the door.'

Samantha's forehead and nose sweated; she could not fathom the repercussions of her mother knowing that she had lit a cigarette. 'I'm just lying, Ma. I'll come down now. You leave,' she blabbered, somehow, while she cleared all the ash with her hands and rinsed under the faucet.

CHAPTER 12

Samantha was already in the meditation hall seated in silence with her eyes closed. She had made her mind to do anything to get her memory back. Andrew was surprised to find her meditating even before he could reach the dorm that morning.

'Impressive,' he softly said as soon as he entered the meditation hall. A smile bloomed at the corner of her lips; she did not open her eyes but continued to concentrate. It felt impossible to get back to the zone of concentration with Andrew's presence. The least she could concentrate was on his footsteps.

'Concentrate on your breathing,' Andrew instructed with gestures. 'Inhale for four seconds and exhale for as long as you can. Keep your focus point on breathing. Think of a quiet place, the air you're breathing in is your happiness; you are being filled with happiness and the air you exhale is your worries, discomforts, and the agony inside. Exhale, push everything out.'

How perfect all his words are, she thought. Samantha slowly started picturing Andrew, his voice, his eyes, his hair which almost touched his eyebrows but did not.

His beard, which gorgeously decorated his jawline, and his lips which had a pink tint. She was surprised to have captured so many details about him without effort. She realized that she had been lately admiring Andrew every time he spoke with her, every time he had cared for and caressed her. Andrew always treated her like a child, like a growing bird in his hands, like a newly woven silk, or like a randomly seen butterfly.

He spoke in a monotone without distracting her concentration. 'Now, breathe to the count of four, three, two...'

'Saarr. Kaaffee.' A short guy who delivered coffee from canteen entered with his high-pitched voice, a hot coffee pot in his hands. Andrew and Samantha jerked as soon as they heard him. Samantha's eyes were wide open; Andrew sighed. 'Come here...' he waved and said, 'there should not be any shouting from tomorrow, okay?'

'Okay, saar,' the man responded in the same tone. They both cracked up finding no improvement. 'No. No voice. Only knock. Just knock on the door, and I'll come and get the coffee, alright?' Andrew enacted the knock with his fist. The short guy repeated the gesture and showed a thumbs up.

Andrew poured some coffee into the cup and held the body of the cup completely with his palms to check if Samantha would be able to hold the temperature. She did not take her eyes off him. The posture of holding the cup had slightly tightened his folded shirt sleeves at the biceps. He had fair complexion, sharp eyes, a sharp nose which was slightly curved at the end but attractive, and a much comforting smile which revealed neatly arranged pearl-like teeth. A smile that was almost covered in this dense beard. He wore a light blue shirt and cream formal pants. Had he been a bit taller, he could've been a supermodel she thought.

'Sam!' Andrew gave a shout which broke her captivate moment.

'Yeah?'

'Here. Have it before it gets cold.' His tone reminded her of the tone of her mother rushing in the mornings while getting ready to school. Samantha asked what she always wondered.

'Hey, Neethu told me that we knew each other before. Is that true?'

'Yes. We do! But, how does she—'

'Ha! It wasn't her. I guessed.'

'Well, in fact what is there to guess? It was me who brought you here, isn't that obvious?'

'Isn't it? It is! But I feel we have known each other since a very long time, I mean, I definitely don't feel like we just met.'

'Might or might not be true.'

'Since when then?' she asked without any delay.

'What?'

'Since when do we know each other?' Her tone was slightly flirtish, as if throwing one of those random pickup lines any school boys would use against girls but she also knew that the feeling was real. Her question had pushed Andrew into thoughts. He sat right next to her whilst he gave her the coffee cup. He sighed, remembering the first time he saw Samantha.

It was a year and a half ago on a spring Sunday afternoon. Andrew had been to a church for the first time ever since he had moved to Bangalore two weeks prior. After the prayer service, he was approached by a few girls.

'Hi, sir, good morning.'

'Hello!' said another.

'Sir, we're collecting funds to feed hungry children, would you like to contribute please?' One of the girls stretched the metal charity box forward, parallel to his face.

'Yea, sure,' he said, grabbing his wallet from the back pocket of his denim. He quickly searched the compartments realizing there was only a hundred rupees note. 'Well, I don't have much in cash now.' His voice trailed off.

'No problem, sir. Whatever is possible for you at the moment.'

'Sure.' He dropped the note into the charity box with a soft smile.

'Sir!' He heard someone call out while he was just about to cross the gates of the church. 'Hi, sir. I'm sorry to bother you. I'm Samantha. I head this initiative camp. Do you have a couple of minutes please?'

'Yes. No problem.'

'Thank you so much. We're running this fundraising camp for homeless children all over Bangalore. Not in the name of any fancy organizations or orphanages. This is a sole initiative. You see, there are thousands of homeless people across, especially kids who die mostly due to hunger or being malnourished. All the charity organizations have a set of volunteers to raise funds or they are anyways associated with constant philanthropists. But these homeless people are too scared to get admitted to any charitable trust homes. So, we've decided to at least start providing them with food. It would be great if you could help.'

'Well, I think what you're doing is great. I really appreciate it. But currently, I don't have cash on me, so—'

'No problem, sir. Thank you so much for your time.'

'Okay.' Thoughts ran in his head for a moment. 'How about...'

'Pardon, sir?'

‘How about next Sunday? Will you guys be here? I really want to contribute.’

‘Yes, sir. This goes on for the entire month. And this is the church we all go to, so we’ll be here most of the weekends.’

‘Great. See you next Sunday, then. What’s your name again?’

‘Samantha,’ she said with a spark in her eyes. ‘And you, sir?’

‘I’m Andrew.’

‘Okay. Thank you so much, sir.’ His soul was nourished with her charm, he felt it even after he reached home.

Andrew had patiently waited for the next Sunday, counting days throughout the week. He was not quite sure if the waiting was to extend his help or to revisit the spark in her eyes. He kept the funds ready by mid-week. On Saturday night, he made sure his beard and hair were intact and mindfully chose his outfit for the next day. On Sunday, he got up way earlier then his alarm would go off and got to the church. His eyes travelled across the whole crowd searching for the charm his soul craved for. While the prayer was midway through he was automatically pulled by a shine from the choir. He was amazed by the natural force that pulled him towards her. He stared at her for several minutes in astonishment. ‘How is this possible?’ he said to himself, experiencing such a force for the first time ever in his life.

'Andrew!' Samantha said, pulling Andrew from the past to the present.

'I thought you were about to tell me something. I'm waiting. Where did you fly away?' she asked, placing her empty cup back on the tray.

'I was just recollecting everything. The first time I met you and all'

'Really?' Her eyes widened with a grin.

'Yeah, feels like yesterday.'

'Come on, tell me.'

'The first time I saw you was in a church. You were heading a team for fundraising camp to feed homeless people all over Bangalore.'

'Fundraising camp?' Her eyes widened.

'Yes, you asked me for funds and I didn't have cash on me that day.'

'And?'

'And… I donated the following week.'

'And?'

'And now, if you let me, I should go to the hospital.'

Samantha rolled her eyes. 'No. Tell me more.'

'Sure, next time.' Andrew left, leaving her eyes sparkling in anticipation.

Andrew had spent that whole day trying to push away the bitter feeling of the day he never wanted to remember again. He could not resist recalling it when he got back home later that day. He was transferred to Chennai for a couple of months and could not visit the church again. Four months earlier, he got back to Bangalore and was curious to revisit the eyes of a charm after two long months. But this time, he only saw her as a walking corpse. Her mother held her hand while they walked. She looked pale and weak. She did not recognise Andrew when their eyes met; her gaze was indifferent. Andrew sensed a lifetime of pain and agony in Samantha's eyes and he could not just let her pass. He gave a quick thought, took his visiting card from his wallet and walked towards them. He extended the card to Layla. 'Please use this for any medical help required.' Layla stared at the card and Andrew, confused.

'I am distributing this to everyone as a mental health awareness. You can call this number for any questions or help. Please ignore otherwise.'

Layla had initially walked past the card with a firm face, but turned back to Andrew within a couple of steps. 'Thank you.' She pulled the card from the middle of his fingers and walked hastily out of the church, pulling Samantha along by grabbing her hand.

'All you need to do when you are angry is count to ten. Think about two things while counting, What does this anger lead to and how severe the situation would look a day after? It can be so silly that you might even laugh at,' said Andrew to a patient who had frequent quarrels dealing with his wife's short temper.

'Okay, Doctor, but how do I make her count?'

'Mr. Suresh, children will not learn the numbers without the teacher chanting them. You start first and make her join.'

'I shall try.'

'Please do. Don't forget to take your medicines. And... is your house air-conditioned?'

'Yes, why?'

'Look, the summer is on top of our head. It is a scorching May. Keep the wife air conditioned always. A cosy and pleasant environment is really important to stay calm.'

The patient acknowledged with a nod and left the room. A nurse slid the next report file onto Andrew's desk. He took a few minutes to thoroughly study the file with a frowned face. He checked the name multiple times remembering it from the church and hoped this to be a different person.

Samantha was brought into the room, her mom and dad holding her hands on either side. Her mom held one of her hands tight, resisting it from her pulling away. Her parents' faces bore frowned eyebrows with their lips curved to the ground. Andrew pointed his right hand at the chairs and said, 'Please take a seat.' He had a constant doctor smile on his face although he was shocked to look at Samantha in even more worse situation. All three sat politely.

'Good morning, Doctor,' wished Victor. Samantha's father adjusted his spectacles. He looked fit for his age, though the silver beard showed him to be older. His eyes laid out all his worries. He looked tense with his unevenly combed hair.

Layla, Samantha's mother, looked devastated with her puffy eyes. They had a ray of hope that things would get better. Samantha looked fierce. She stared at each and everything on the table. Her gaze shuffled rapidly; she constantly bit her nails.

'Yes, I have read the profile. How are things now? How are you doing, Samantha, right?' Andrew felt silly to re-confirm the name of the person he was well aware of. She did not respond though she heard the question; rather she chose not to. 'Well, I want you two to wait outside. Let me have a small chat with Samantha in person.' Samantha clenched her mother's saree and tried to stand along when her mom and dad stood to leave.

'Sit. The doctor will talk to you,' said her mother, pushing her gently against the chair.

Andrew waited until they left the room completely. 'Hi, can you hear me?' She looked at Andrew for a brief minute without a response. 'Do u remember me?' he asked with a bit of hope. She did not respond. 'Never mind. How are you, Samantha?' She stared at him with rage.

Andrew noticed her looking really sleep deprived and sick. His heart sank to see her this way. 'How are you? Tell me whatever it is. The sooner you tell, the sooner you can leave.' He waited. 'Do you want some water?'

She nodded.

He opened the lid of the plastic bottle and passed it over to her. 'Great!' He waited a few moments. 'Samantha, consider me as a friend. Tell me how you feel, would you?'

'I hate… I hate this place. Why should I even be here? Ma!' she screamed.

'Sure. But, do you know what place this is? People come here for various reasons like if they are unable to sleep, if they don't have friends, if they fail an exam, or if they break up with their partners, and so on. I'm pretty sure you have one of these problems. I will surely help. Now, what is it?' Andrew noticed her being anxious. 'Okay. Firstly, shall we count to ten together? Starting one, two, three…' He started counting with regular intervals, expecting her to join. She did not utter a word.

'Eight, nine, ten. Okay, good.' He grabbed a few tools and continued talking, 'We shall call your parents inside if you do this exercise with me. Now, please can you tell me what is written on the white side of this cube?' Andrew handed over the Rubik's cube to her which had a word on each side. She turned the misplaced top row of white side to match the same colour and said, 'Calm.'

'Good and on the yellow side?' She rotated the cube slowly and stared at the words on the yellow side without saying anything. 'Parents are waiting,' he reminded.

She gasped and said, 'Rest.'

'Great! Thank you for doing that. Now, shall we talk about something non-physical. How are you feeling? What is your ultimate feeling right now?' Her lips tightened, eyes filled with tears that were about to overflow, but she stayed quiet. 'Tell me what is bothering you. Is it any issues at college or with your friends... Or is it about your relationship? Let's solve it together. Let's not tell your parents about it. Deal? I can help you. Samantha, trust me. I can see a lot of pain in those eyes'

'Nonsense. I don't need your help. You can't help me.' Her tears jumped while she shook her head.

'Okay, don't take my help. But wouldn't you want to have a chat about it? It can make you feel lighter at least.'

'I can't feel light. Not in this life, because I killed my brother,' she said with her sight and tone stable.

Andrew re-experienced the jolt he had earlier. He could not go any further with his thoughts. The thought being more attached to him did rewind again. 'I killed my brother,' she had said, like a criminal confessing the crime after several interrogation sessions. Andrew had no idea what she was talking about; rather he did not expect or experienced anything like this before.

'Wha...what?'

'I KILLED MY BROTHER!' Samantha cried out. 'I didn't do it on purpose. But, how should I tell this to Mom and Dad? It was all my fault.' Samantha spoke only half of the words with running tears. She did not care where she was and with whom she was talking to. All she knew was that she needed to vent her agony.

Andrew reached her instantly and tried to console. 'It's okay.. it's okay, Samantha... Breathe.'

'It was all my fault...' Samantha cried again.

'I understand. I'm so sorry but you're hurting yourself a lot. This is not good. It is not your fault, Samantha. Listen to me. Please, stop crying. I want you to talk to me.' Andrew felt this was a pain she bore in herself not sharing with anyone. 'Did you tell your parents about this?'

'No...' She broke down. Her face had turned all pink. 'I don't want them to hate me for doing this.'

'Okay...will you tell me what happened right from the beginning?'

CHAPTER 13

7 Months Before

It was 11:20 am when Samantha finally decided to get off her bed. She dragged herself to the kitchen and found her mom had already started her preparation for lunch.

'Coffee will take ten minutes,' she said even before Samantha could ask for it.

'I appreciate your proactiveness.' She patted her mother's shoulders.

'Meanwhile, get coffee cups from Bunny's room and ask if he needs another cup of coffee.'

'Bunny! Is he home? On a weekday!' She jumped at once. 'This dude is early to work and late home. It has been three days since I've seen him,' she tutted.

'He's not keeping well. He keeps telling me that his head hurts. I tried giving him tablets and several rounds of coffee, but nothing seems to work.' Her mother's lips were drawn down.

'Oh! That is something I need to tackle with, let me get rid of it, Mother.'

'Go, go chat with him.'

Samantha felt a sort of calmness at home. *I think the ambiance is calling for it*, she thought. She sneaked onto the steps without making a sound, planning to scare him. The door of his room was half-open. Samantha climbed only at the corner of every step, pushing herself against the wall. Okay! Push the door and shout simultaneously. She revised the plan in her head. I am gonna reset the scare level which he never compromised on. The recent experience of the scare game had got Samantha still startled.

She had pushed the doorknob of Simon's room to check if he was available that night, and Simon grabbed her wrist, slowly from behind the door. "Scary pig. Scary pig," he had shouted, scaring the shit out of her. *It's my turn dear brother*, she thought.

She took a deep breath to shout as loud as possible. 'BOOOO!' she screamed while she hustled past the door as swiftly as possible. She heard a cracking sound of chinaware resonating along with her voice. She failed to picture what was happening; only after a moment did she realize that she actually messed up big time. Simon had laid all his architectural plans on the floor beside his bed, maybe to have a bird's eye view. He'd placed two of the paperweights on each of the left corners, grouped markers and highlighters were placed them on the bottom right corner, and a coffee cup was placed on the top right corner of the sheet, which is close to the door. Both Simon and Samantha stared at the coffee-stained sheets and the scattered pieces of the cup. Simon had never finished his coffee completely. Out of habit, he always left close to two sips at the bottom of his cup. The next thing she knew was a bang on her cheek. She reached for her cheek instantly, 'Ouch! My ear hurts,' she murmured.

'Are you out of your mind?' He was fuming out of rage, his eyes turning red and nostrils flared. 'Can't you act sensible? You have no idea how important these are. Don't you dare enter my room again. Get lost!' Simon closed his eyes tight, pinching the bridge of his nose.

Samantha's eyes emerged a rush of tears, and her cheek bore reddish traces of his palm. She felt the connections between her ear, jaw, and brain were displaced someway. She quickly went to her room and locked herself inside. How could he shout at me like that; how could he treat me like a useless person; how could he slap me; how could he hurt me both physically and emotionally? Are those papers more important than me and my feelings? This is something he never done to me... I have never been so hard on him, whatever he did. She held her hurt pink cheek whilst tears continued to flow, half due to pain and the rest in rage. She lay on her bed grinding her teeth, not being able to digest what had just happened. 'I hate him,' she said louder to satisfy her ego. 'I will never talk to him! Ever!' She replayed the whole episode again and again regretting having scared him at that moment. The more she thought about him slapping her, the more she hated him. The fact that there was no sign of regret on his face fed her ego more. She wondered about the importance of that coffee-stained architect plan. She wiped her tears by rubbing her palms hard against her sore cheeks.

She grabbed her phone in an attempt to deviate her mind. She swiped away the lined-up notifications from various applications one-by-one. Her thumb halted while she reached the one from WhatsApp. It was a message from her college group. It read, "'RIDE ON HIGH'. Nominate yourself if you think you can beat it! Else bet it off. The winner gets twenty thousand and a free bike service."

This was a well-known routine in their college. Every quarter, there was a track set through one of the highways in the city where the nominated people race and the others bet on their favorite rider. At that moment, Samantha's pride peaked and she decided she should nominate Simon for the race. She could not decide if she was doing it in anger, as that would no way make him regret what he did to her, but she knew there were a couple of riders who always won the race and would even win this race. Nominating her brother to lose would at least hit right on his ego. She nominated Simon for the race and sent him the link quoting, 'I bet you lose!' She found immediate relief in doing it.

While she thought that he would not even care to glance at her message, she received a response. 'Sure! Can't wait.'

'Seriously!' she murmured, rolling her eyes.

Her imagination draw her onto the roads. Instantly, she could picture him throttling the bike, overtaking the opponent effortlessly, and winning the race. She pictured him coming to her after the race and calling out, 'LOSER'. She was scared that all that she'd imagined would come true. What will I do then? What if he demands something I can't afford to get him? She avoided leaving her room and spent almost the whole day with her phone and desktop.

Her mom visited a couple of times to give her food. 'Sam, aren't you going to come out? He might have been in some office tension, you shouldn't have done it in the first place, right?' she said the second time she visited. Mrs. Layla's words did not convince her, rather they only hurt her more. *Even mom is not ready to back me up*, she thought.

'I don't wanna talk to anyone. Please go. I'm not coming,' she said with a frown. The thought of the race the day after kept haunting her. She felt excited, upset, and nervous altogether. She heard the doorknob unlocking and doubted it was her mother again. She shut her eyes tight, pretending to sleep as soon as she heard the door open. She felt Simon's rough palms against her cheek caressing. Her heart raced in anger but she continued to pretend to be asleep. Simon picked at the comforter, whispering 'I'm sorry,' while he wrapped it around her.

'I bet you'll lose the race,' she said, keeping her eyes shut.

'Ok, dear! Get some sleep now.' He smiled.

Samantha stood in the scorching sun amongst the college crowd who were cheering for their own heroes. Unlike others, she was not there to support anyone. She wanted to witness her brother lose. At least once in her lifetime, she was just expecting to take revenge, the answer for her ego, justice for her hurt. Most of the crowd screamed while the tall racer entered. He was known to win any bike challenge he had participated in so far. 'Look, he bought a brand-new bike with all the money he won,' someone screamed from the crowd. He looked sturdy and reckless. He didn't seem to care about any damage he might get if something had to happen. It seemed as if his bike and the roads were intimidated by him.

Two other racers entered the lane with leather jackets and helmets in their hands. It was understood from the attire that they were amongst the competing racers. She looked around to find Simon in the vicinity. She, for a moment, hoped that he would not turn up to the race, not compete with these people who were almost professionals.

A tall girl wearing black jeans and a body-hugging black polo came in front of the crowd with a printed sheet in her hand. She waved to the crowd, showing the white sheets. The noise gradually calmed down as she spoke. 'The race will start from the Vittal Mallya road, following the Bangalore - Mysore expressway. The midpoint is at the NICE toll plaza. The racers will have to collect their flags from the midpoint and reach the start point to finish the lap. The maximum time to reach is forty minutes, and the minimum is how long the fastest racer will take. Of course, the one who returns first will win,' she declared.

That was a route where there wouldn't be a minute without a lorry passing by. Samantha only then knew the entire route of it and realized it was a big deal. The traffic, lorries passing by, signals, the tall guy who always won... Everything occurred to her right at once. She knew that it wasn't a small trap she had pushed her brother into, nothing less than an elephant trap. At that moment, the last thing she wished was for Simon to arrive.

As always, her wish collapsed right away. She saw Simon next to a friend, listening to his words carefully. His friend was guiding him on the route to take as he spoke with his hands raised in the air and pointing at directions. He was wearing his hard-souled woodland shoes, dark blue jeans, and a red T-shirt, no jacket. Whilst she dreadfully stared at Simon, his eyes turned to look at her as though he heard her calling.

Samantha looked away, not being able to meet his eyes. She heard her phone ring and reached into her pocket. Her jaw clenched and palms sweated looking at Simon's name on the screen. She did not have the courage to pick up that call. She somehow believed that he would finish the race and thought she could talk to him then.

And that he would look at her with his brave triumph. No one traveling by that path would be aware of a race happening; there would be no sign boards nor any stalls in between; reasons like traffic and signals were not agreed upon. The racer was supposed to get the flag from the people over 17.5 km away from the starting point and should get back to the same spot where they had started. The one who comes back first wins the race. There were many cases of accidents that happened in the past which were only considered general road accidents, and not part of the race.

All the racers put their helmets and gloves on tight. Bikes were throttled, raising mud into the air, adding to the pollution that was already there. Simon had also throttled his Yamaha R15, matching the tempo. Samantha could clearly differentiate the noise her brother's bike made out of all the six bikes that were racing. A girl with red-colored hair stood in front of all the racers with a white flag. She was also wearing a black polo and only then Samantha learned that all the organizers of the race, both men and women, wore black polos. A tall muscular guy stood on the right side of the racers with a whistle in his hand. The crowd shouted louder when the guy with the whistle raised his hand. He shouted, 'The race is about to begin!"

Samantha looked for Simon, peering over the top of various heads, and could view only the back seat and a bit of his hair. The guy with the whistle counted down, 'three, two, and GO!', then he blew the whistle. The lean girl at the centre waved the white flag down as soon as she heard the whistle. The bikes sped off, making the whole place fogged with smoke and dust. Samantha's eyes were right on Simon's bike as he passed through. She stood right there, did not look around, did not move an inch, and could not think about anything but her brother returning. She tapped her right foot rapidly, picturing him racing back straight to the starting point with a wide smile. She did not expect her brother to win the race, but just to come back safe.

Nearly fifteen minutes after the race had started, she saw a loaded mini truck with a damaged vehicle. She glanced harder, half believing that was not Simon's bike, but she could not trust her eyes. She tried to run further and check the number plate or the stickering of his name on the tail light. The truck crossed the signal and took a left. Samantha stopped herself in the middle of one side of the two-way lane, convincing herself that she hadn't seen her brother's bike. But her heart shook when she listened to the sirens from far away. She thrived through the crowd and ran against the vehicles coming toward her, needing to check who had been in an accident. All at once, when she thought she saw an ambulance in the distance, she felt a bang on her right hip and flew in the air before she could confirm what she was looking at.

CHAPTER 14

BANGALORE

5 Months Before

Thoughts are powerful. Whilst they are powerful enough to make us believe in something that is not true, it is still in our control what we believe.

Samantha believed that her brother was still with her. She spent most of her time in Simon's room. She lit a cigarette whenever she thought she needed fuel for a memory rush, which she craved every single day. As the evoking smoke was inhaled passively, Simon's memories were unveiled in front of her eyes, which she dwelled upon for hours together. She spent less time with her family; she joined them precisely only at the time of their meals. She ate less, she often complained the food was too salty or spicy for her liking and walked away.

Victor, however, tried to spend at least some time each day to understand what her ideas were and to restart her life. He was worried that Samantha's life was at standstill after her brother's passing. He tried inviting her to play badminton, which was her favorite pastime with her brother, which she always denied. Once when Samantha had burned all the available cigarettes in Simon's room, she urged herself to get more. The first thought on her mind was how to get a new pack of cigarettes. She religiously believed that cigarettes were the path that led to her gone brother. She thought that that was the only way she could connect with her brother again.

'Sam, do you have five minutes to spend? I need to talk,' Victor asked when she was walking back to her room. Samantha gave a nod, with utmost difficulty agreeing to spend the hardest five minutes thinking about something other than how to get a new cigarette pack.

'Did you decide when you're going to resume your college?' He looked straight into her eyes, confronting her. He had asked Samantha to choose between two options which rich kids would do just to pass their time. The first was to take up a new course in Japan where his friend's daughter was studying, just so they could have an eye on Samantha. The latter was to go on a holiday for a few days and get transferred to a different college anywhere in India to finish the final year of a bachelor's in social work. Victor believed that the deviation of her mood for a short period would get her started with her career without much pressure.

Samantha struggled to recollect what Victor had said the previous day. 'Options?' she asked with a confused face.

'Japan or India?' he repeated, grinding his teeth.

Samantha felt strange, she felt like she was hearing the options for the first time. She was, however, clear on what she wanted to do. 'I don't wanna go anywhere.' She carelessly looked away.

'What else? Do you want to go anywhere else, for some change?'

'Nope. I'm fine being home.'

'Samantha!' His tone went higher. 'I know we've had a loss. It is a tremendous loss for our entire family. We don't want you to dwell in it, leaving your own life aside. Look, we want you to be happy. That is the only reason for asking you to leave this house, go somewhere, get some fresh air, and come back lively. We all shouldn't be buried in sadness.' Every word from Victor reminded her of the fact that Simon was no more. Every time it was said out loud, the truth stabbed her heart. She felt breathless. She could not take the fact that her parents were getting over the loss or that they were prepared to get over it already.

'Will you please stop it?' Samantha screamed with her eyes closed. 'Bunny is still here. He is with us. He sees what we all are doing. He still lives with us; can't you feel it? You're all ready to forget what has happened? To forget him? Never ever say that we've lost him.' She burst into tears in rage. Samantha could not stay in that place anymore. She took a five hundred rupee note from her desk, wore a hoodie, and walked out fiercely. Her parents did not stop her, nor did they ask any questions.

She walked in search of a store where she could get cigarettes. She entered a supermarket where she could pick those up by herself without having to ask the shopkeeper. She remembered the packaging but had never noticed the name. She quickly picked up a similar cigarette pack from the counter and headed toward the billing area. She kept pulling the hoodie over her head, covering her face. There she saw Mr. Murthy, Victor's badminton partner. Samantha took a turnabout as soon as she saw her father's dear friend. Mr. Murthy encountering her with a cigarette pack in hand was the last thing she would want to happen.

She hid herself in a section that was not directly visible from the billing area. She picked up a kid's storybook from the stationary section and peered at the billing counter from behind it. Mr. Murthy was still there billing his groceries, having a nice prolonged chat with the person in the billing area. *Seems like he's getting the whole store billed*, she thought, passing her time with the rest of the stationery items. She remembered how she used to flick the peanut and carrot-shaped erasers from her brother's stationery and later denied the blame. Her hands trembled when she saw Mr. Murthy coming towards the stationery section. She shoved the cigarette pack behind the stacked books.

'Samantha?' His voice startled her as she stood facing the wall with a random book in her hand.

She turned, pretending to be pleasantly surprised and said, 'Hi, uncle!'

'Samantha! I was just doubting if it was you. I'm extremely sorry for the loss, dear.' He hugged her warmly. Yes, it is a loss! Should I say that or should I go with, it's okay? But I'm really not okay. Samantha did not know how to respond. She could only look down at the shiny floor trying not to spill out any tears. 'I spoke with your dad the other day. Just a few words, how is he now?'

'Yeah, he's okay.'

'Alright, girl. Don't stress out. God will be with you!' He touched the tip of her head with his cupped palm and left. Samantha gave a formal smile as he walked away. She repeated the phrase, 'God'll be with you!' in her head. Why would God take back a part of me and be with me to comfort me? She did not take the hidden cigarette pack, for she knew that if she purchased cigarettes here, the information would slide on to Mr. Murthy as smooth as air, from there to her dad, and eventually to her mother which could be the end of the world.

Samantha left the store right after Mr. Murthy. She was certain that she couldn't get cigarettes in her locality. While she dragged her body back home with uncertain steps, she heard a faint voice, 'Hey, Sammy!' A tall guy came running towards her. Samantha had to lift her head higher than usual to meet his eyes. She frowned initially but recognized him in a few seconds. She recollected all their memories, but barely remembered his name.

'Hi...' She scratched her forehead.

'Varun. Dude… did you forget college guys already?' the tall guy said with an enthusiastic voice. Varun, yes, Varun! Radha's boyfriend.

'Yea, Varun. No, I didn't forget. Just… But you look different. With more hair and beard.'

'Oh yea, no college, no work, no rules. You know...' He combed the dense hair falling on his face with his fingers. She nodded. 'I recognized you from far away and came running. Glad I got to see you after such a long time. Okay then... I'll see you around.' He giggled.

'Okay!' She waved. Lots of memories hit her head. Radha and Samantha were close friends until the second year. The two along with Varun had bunked many classes and had gone to the movies or to one of their houses just to spend some fun time together. Samantha had not seen Varun since she got separated from Radha.

'Sammy!' She heard Varun screaming again.

'Hey, all fine?' she asked.

'Yeah, wanted to give you my number,' he panted.

'Sure' She reached into her pockets immediately, 'Oh no. I think I didn't bring my phone.' She shrugged.

'It's okay. I can write it in a chit.' He checked his bag, which almost looked empty, for a piece of paper and a pen. 'I'm glad I ran into you, Sammy. We all used to have great fun, remember? I really miss those days.' He conversed while he searched for the pen. 'I think I've lost my pen. Well, I saw a store. Can you go there with me? It won't take much time.'

'No problem.' She smiled calmly, both of them walking towards the store slowly. The idea of getting a cigarette pack was still hanging on top of her head. She gave it a brief thought. 'I miss those days too! Those were really fun. If not for my fight with Radha, we would've been in touch,' Samantha tutted.

'You fought with her? I don't think that's true. She is the one who starts fights.' He smirked.

'Don't you know? I can't believe she didn't even mention me.'

'We never had a conversation, dude. We broke up right after the fourth semester.'

'Really?' Samantha touched her right temple. 'No friend, no love, She would've gone through a tough time' said Samantha.

'I have no idea. She shut me out completely from her world. Okay, you wait here, I'll go get a pen'

'Varun!' she called urgently. 'If you don't mind, can you...' She dragged her words.

'what is it?'

'Can you– I don't know if I can ask you this.'

'No issues, dude. Just temme what you need?'

'Can you get me a cigarette pack?' Samantha finally asked. Varun was dumbfounded for a nanosecond, and his eyes wouldn't blink. His smile was drawn wide, eventually putting a curve on his face. 'Dude, you're awesome! What do you smoke?' he asked more casually.

She was embarrassed by his decibel. 'No. I don't smoke.' She put her face towards the ground.

'Oh, chill. Never mind. Which one should I get?'

'Well, it has golden packaging. I'm not sure of the name.'

'Okay, I'll try my best.' Varun got her the golden pack that she had asked for along with his number written on the bill. 'Here you go, call me if you need anything.'

'Thanks, man! This is a great help, really.' She tilted her head to his kindness and they left, going separate ways. Samantha found a bit of her heart in relief after meeting Varun. Despite the hesitation, she knew for sure that asking him for a favour was her last resort.

She spent the rest of the day visiting all the pictures that were taken with Simon. She admired the fullness of his smile that was constant. His smile was content. She couldn't recall the last time they'd both had such a laugh together. Their pictures gave her an intense nostalgic twirl. Growing up takes away many things from us that we don't even realize. She mused upon each and every snap longer than usual.

'Dear...' called Layla, entering the room. Samantha was startled, breaking out of her thoughts. She closed the album swiftly within a blink before her mother could notice. 'We had dinner. Shall I get it here for you?'

'No. I'm not hungry.'

'Sam, I... I'm feeling scared looking at you.' She sat on the outer corner of the bed opposite Samantha and continued talking, 'I don't know. I still cannot believe that Simon has left us. And now, all we have is you. We want you to be happy, and healthy, to be strong mentally and physically to tackle life as it comes. You should finish college and be independent. Do what you love to do. Sam, your father and I are pretty sure of one thing. There shouldn't be a single situation where you think that things could've been better only if Simon were to be alive. We hope you understand that.' Layla couldn't hold her tears back, she broke down.

Samantha did not move; she didn't even cut her gaze off of her mother. Her stare was constant and indifferent.

'Are you even listening to me? Will you assure me that? Huh?' Layla wiped her eyes.

'No!' Samantha's voice was steady, 'I think you're unreasonable, Ma. Insensitive or even cruel. You sound like you never had a son at all. How could you, Ma? How could you talk like that.'

'Oh baby, I understand...'

'No, you don't. Bunny is not just my brother; he guided me and protected me more than you guys did. I cannot forget all of those moments and just be happy. You didn't want me to feel what? That things would've been better if Bunny had been here? I already feel it, Ma. I feel that way for every fleeting moment. No one—no one can change it. No one can make my life better.'

When Samantha came home from the hospital, the day after Simon died, she was left with only his picture decorated with flowers in the living room. She witnessed the disconsolate house, the saddened flowers, the screaming curtains, the dumb people, the depressing odour from the incense sticks, and Simon's picture. She noticed everything slowly changed in just a week. People gained voices that spoke things not related to Simon, the screaming curtains were consciously changed and tied, the flowers and incense sticks which bore most of the sorrow were removed, and the picture climbed onto a special frame out of reach. Samantha denied changing, improving, or recovering. She denied moving on and despised everything that did.

Samantha joined the dining table for lunch the next day to make up for the quarrel the previous night. Victor's and Layla's faces lit up with her presence.

'Serve. Serve hot,' Victor instructed Layla.

Samantha's stomach growled looking at the piping hot rice, dal, and cauliflower roast neatly arranged as a platter. Samantha took the metal spoon in to her hand, she herself felt it had been quite some time since she'd held the spoon between her fingers. She took her first bite, realizing how well her mother cooked.

'So, did you think about what I asked you last night?' Victor said, taking his first bite.

'Victor!' Layla said with her stern voice.

'Wait,' he said to Layla and continued talking, 'Listen, Sam. I am not forcing you. I see that you are not even considering to think about it. I want you to think. The Japan admission closes tomorrow. Think about the options, think about your future—'

'Victor, let her eat. Let's talk later.'

'I am not expecting an answer right away. Let me know by tonight.'

'I am not going anywhere,' Samantha said, not looking at him.

Victor sighed. 'Okay! You need not leave the house. At least do something here. Staying home. Do you want home tutors? I can arrange them.' Victor had some hope about the home tutorials.

Layla sensed the pressure Samantha would be going through and tried to back her up. 'Victor, enough. I think she can take her time to decide on this.'

'There is no time, Layla. Let me talk.'

'Alright. But not now. Not at the table.'

'All her batch mates have finished college. Most of them have secured jobs. It has been three months. I see no improvement in this house.'

'Victor. Why are you rushing. What for? If she wants to stay home, she will. I think we should leave her for now.'

'You don't understand what I'm trying to do.'

'I don't want to. I cannot stay calm looking at this. It's you who is not understanding.'

'Do you think she is your daughter alone? I'm her father and I have all rights to decide on her future.'

'Stop,' Samantha said under her breath, her face almost fumed.

'That's not what I meant—'

'STOP!' she screamed as loud as she could. 'I will do whatever you want me to do, please don't fight like this, please!' She left her meal, went back to her room, and slammed the door. She wondered how Simon would have dealt with the situation and realized his absence was the cause of everything happening. Samantha's eyes were struck by the picture that hung on the wall. It was a picture taken when Victor bought his first camera. Samantha was seven and Simon was thirteen. The picture was an early morning click of both sleepy faces; Samantha stuck her tongue carelessly while Simon read through the specifications from the camera's pamphlet. Samantha closed her eyes to concentrate. She tried hard to remember the events while the picture was clicked. She barely remembered anything from that morning.

She picked up a pen that was lying around and pushed her thumb against the nib. Tears rolled down for all the already forgotten memories with her brother. She was drawn towards fluttering paper on her writing table. It looked as if the sunlight emerged from the middle of the curtains to focus on the piece of chit. She stared at it for several minutes, recalling it was the bill that had Varun's number on it. She took it delicately into her hands and dialled the number on her phone. She hesitated before dabbing on the call icon. She shuddered, hearing her mother's voice from the kitchen, changing her mind and hovering her thumb from 'Call' to 'Add new contact'.

CHAPTER 15

CHENNAI

Samantha did not blink. Her eyes opened wider than usual, reflecting the wide spread of lights, and her stomach filled with butterflies. It was probably the first time Andrew witnessed happiness on her face. Her lips were wider, showing all her teeth.

She swivelled all around the place to capture the multi-coloured lights, different types of people, various food stalls, and importantly, the gigantic Ferris wheel. She was reminded of when she and Simon sat in one of those compartments, which hung at right geometrical points all across the wheel, with their hands clenched while they both swung down sitting next to each other. She held Andrew's hand like a kid and raised the other into the sky pointing at the rotating wheel. Her eyes shone and her mouth widened into a grin. She did not speak a word to convey her urge.

From the highest point of the wheel, the city seemed like a starry sky laid on the ground, shining by reflecting the light from the moon. She blinked once to capture the scenery in her heart forever. Her stomach tickled and her eyes shut automatically while they descended down. She held Andrew's hands as tightly as she would have held Simon's.

They took a stroll after the adventurous ride. Her eyes gazed upon the children playing around. A person's eye will always be in search of something one is longing for. How lucky these kids were. She imagined Simon and herself amongst the children who were playing without worrying about anything else in this world. A smile appeared on her face and faded within seconds due to a sudden sensation.

A discomfort suddenly struck her from nowhere. Her eyes widened as she sniffed harder. She hastily turned all around, trying to locate the origin of this familiar smell. She stood in the middle of the food stalls, not realizing that she was blocking the way. Her eyes landed on the group of men who were smoking at one corner far from the food stalls. Her eyes narrowed instinctively, and glitched scenes of her past flashed in her head without coherence. Cigarettes, dense smoke, screams, darkness, blood, and Simon. She was partially paralyzed by the unceasingly disturbing prompts in her head. She wondered where these were emerging from.

Andrew gently nudged her back, both his hands holding ice cream. 'I asked you to sit there, remember?' He rolled his eyes towards the concrete bench that was a few feet away. He sensed that something was wrong by the expression on her face.

'Are you okay? Did someone bother you?' he asked, looking around.

Samantha kept her sight constant on the people smoking, without moving an inch away. 'Sam!' Andrew cried, realizing what happened. He immediately dropped an ice cream from one hand and dragged her out of that place.

He made her sit in the car, with the other ice cream she'd asked for. 'Are you okay?' he asked trying to catch her eyes. She slowly nodded, still haunted by the glitched memories. 'Eat, it's melting.' It seemed as if she was melting the ice cream with her staring eyes. A drop dripped onto her hand, Andrew immediately took a tissue and wiped it off. 'Please eat,' he said with a twinkle in his eyes.

She slowly grabbed the melting peak of ice cream with her lips. Andrew felt happy looking at her eat. He stared at the bit of ice cream that was stuck on the top right of her upper lip, next to a mole. 'Uh… some… '

'What?' she asked.

'Vanilla... mole.'

'What?'

'There is some ice cream on your vanilla. Oh, no. No, no. There is some vanilla on your mole.' He giggled and approached slowly with his pointed finger. Samantha's face fumed, experiencing the unusually close distance that she could feel his breath.

‘Tissue,’ she snapped.

‘Oh, yes. Tissue.’ He regretted his thought of using his finger to wipe the ice cream and handed the tissue over to her. They both exchanged smiles, feeling the tension of the moment.

‘What is that?’ she asked about the package that was sitting on the dashboard.

‘That’s some food. I ordered along with the ice cream for you to eat. I think it wasn’t an appropriate place to eat.’

‘Shall we give it to someone?’ she asked without hesitation.

‘To whom?’

‘To anyone who needs it.’

‘Well, I appreciate that. But it’s for you. I mean, shall I get you something else?’

‘No. don’t worry about it. Neethu would’ve picked up dinner for me.’

‘Alright. Whatever you wish.’

On their way back, they found a tiny hut made of hay. Andrew gave the parcel to Samantha. ‘Here you go,’ he said with a kind smile.

Samantha walked slowly to find an old lady sitting with a dog at the entrance of the poorly lighted hut. ‘I’ve got some food for you. Please eat.’ She handed the package hesitantly.

'Thank you! God bless you kid.'

Samantha felt heartfully happy. The smile on her face persisted throughout their journey back. Some things as a person would never change Andrew thought, recalling the collection of charity funds. They both were quite carried away by random small talks, overcoming the disturbing scenes of her past.

CHAPTER 16

BANGALORE

4 months before

'I have a set of pamphlets kept here, please share amongst yourselves. Make sure everyone gets it.' The instructor gestured to pass on the pamphlets to the back benches. 'This sheet has a variety of projects that you can choose from. Guys, now you need to pay attention in choosing yours, because your project carries most of the weightage while you're being evaluated.' He looked deep into the students' eyes. He was tall, with slim hands and legs but a tiny pot belly. He wore a pair of loose-bottomed formal pants, a shirt that urges to be torn at the middle of his belly, and an overcoat.

Samantha had agreed to continue the final year in the same college she'd done the first two. She felt as strange as being in a forest with no familiar face around. Her eyes captured the instructor explaining things by moving his hands in and out, but none of his words could reach her brain. She examined various men across the room to find if anyone resembled her brother, if anyone had his smile, his gait, or his hairstyle, at the least. She kicked the ground under the bench several times, breathing heavily. She panted, feeling claustrophobic. She felt each and every atom of her body protesting to get out of that place. She revisited Varun's words loud and clear, to call him whenever she needed help.

Varun!

She dug through her bag roughly for the bill which had the phone number. She paused and recalled that she had saved his number the other day. In her phone's contact list, she had saved the number as 'Var'.

Hi, need help!

She held her phone under the desk. Her gaze shuffled between the tutor and the phone screen, expecting a response.

Sure. but who is this?

The response jolted her. Did he forget me already? She frowned. Oh, damn! She hurriedly typed an answer.

Oh, so sorry! This is Samantha. College!

Yes… How are you?

Not really well. I need help. I'm stuck in college. Need to get out.

What? Which college? Are you still studying?

The same college we studied in. Too many questions. Can you come now?

Oops. Just wanted to know if anything serious. I'll be there in fifteen.

Thanks.

She sighed knowing she would be out of that room soon. Remembering the days when Simon used to pick her up from college made her forget where she was. Her phone rang exactly in seventeen minutes. She missed the first call wondering how to get out of that room; she received another call within a few seconds. She approached the lecturer hurriedly with her bag. 'It's an urgent call, have to take it.' The lecturer who was interrupted abruptly, briefly looked at her and the phone in her hand and finally pointed at the entrance to leave. She walked as fast as possible.

'Hello?'

'I'm at the entrance. Where are you?' the voice from the phone cried.

'I'm coming. You stay there.'

He grinned as soon as he saw her. 'Hi, thought you wouldn't call me.'

'Sorry to disturb you, But I couldn't stay there. Also, couldn't think of anyone else.'

'No problem, thank God the college was nearby. So, what was the problem? Okay, wait. Be honest and temme how many backlogs you have?'

'Yeah, I didn't finish the last semester. Now, I don't understand a single word

'Wha....what?' Varun turned his torso completely away from the road to give a weird look at Samantha. 'You don't understand? As far as I remember, it was you who used to explain things to us. Remember?' He pointed at his head with his left hand and rode only by accelerating. Samantha did not bother to answer and kept looking at the passing vehicles.

'You could've finished it in April. It was lucky, you know. I cleared all my six papers then.' Varun spoke again after a moment. 'It's okay, where do we go now? Or should I drop you home?'

'NO!' She denied the idea of going home right away.

'Wow! Thanks for making me understand that answers can also be loud and clear.' He smiled at his sarcasm. 'What about coffee?' He did not receive a response as before. Varun took that as a yes since there was no denial.

They both settled at a nearby coffee shop, at a two-seater table which was opposite a television. Varun had ordered a cappuccino for both of them, not risking a response to another question. 'Are you alright, Sammy? I see, you've changed a lot. I mean, you know... not a chatterbox anymore.'

She did not seem to care about any of his comments, she kept looking at the news channel running on television.

'And yea... why didn't you finish college?' He looked into her eyes, resting his chin on his left hand. 'Why did you call me if you don't want to talk to me?'

Samantha looked at Varun for a brief moment and asked, 'Do you smoke?'

Varun cracked up laughing 'Dude...you're crazy!' Samantha did not seem as crazy as her words were to Varun. He believed something was wrong with her. She did not spill a word while they finished their coffee. They walked to the smoking zone after coffee. He reached into his pocket to take a cigarette packet, flipped the top of the pack with his pointing finger, pushed a cigarette on top with his thumb, and held it with the tip of his lips. He did it seamlessly. He pushed another cigarette out of the pack in the same way and pointed toward Samantha. She shook her head vigorously. Varun shrugged, keeping the pack back in his pocket.

'I thought you smoke.' The cigarette dangled at one corner of his lips while he spoke.

'I told you, I don't.'

She felt exactly like when she and her brother had a silly talk on their balcony where Simon smoked and Samantha accompanied him.

The next day when Samantha went to college, she was used to the crowd around her. She sat at the same place she opted for the previous day. She was not feeling good about being around many people but she forced herself to stay. She ground her teeth, bit her nails, tapped her feet, stared at the professor for no reason, and was lost in a void for most of the time. She somehow figured that the professor was just selling the projects to students from his project centre.

'Wouldn't be necessary,' she answered when she was asked to get one. She received a call from Varun at the same time she had called him the previous day.

'Hello,' she answered without being bothered about the professor.

'Hey, at college?'

'Yes'

'Need rescued?'

'Sure!' The conversation was more mutual. It seemed like Samantha already knew that Varun would call, and that Varun was already aware that she wanted his help. He took her to the same coffee shop. Samantha stayed quiet the same way she did the previous day. This time Varun had decided to put his face down without speaking a word or bothering much.

'Is everything okay?' she asked.

'You asking me?'

'Yes.'

'Well, I'm just trying to be you for some time.' He giggled. She breathed hard at his joke.' Sammy! I know, I can sense if something is not okay. Whatever it might be, I'll try to help.'

'I am fine. I don't need help,' Samantha responded firmly.

Varun throttled his bike to the middle of a dead-end street. The lane was quiet with not many people around. One woman was taking a pile of neatly folded laundry into an apartment, most of the doors were shut, and an old man was selling some fruits on a tricycle headed to the opposite street. Everyone seemed to mind their own business. Varun took Samantha into an old building through the narrow staircase. Her steps were filled with uncertainty.

'What is this place? Where are we going?'

'Shush! This is where I smoke. Come, you'll like it,' he whispered.

It was around 6.40 in the evening when the two went to the terrace. The place smelled weird to her, like a pile of wood burning up. She was unsure if she really liked the place. Varun took her to his usual spot, into the unmaintained, dry concrete water tank. She felt bizarre entering the cave-like tank but thought it was a perfect fit for her mood. A little solo place where she could be herself. There were people outside the tank, but it was quiet; people over there did not talk much, only smoked.

Samantha liked the vibe they all had, people in silos not disturbing anyone. The evening breeze calmed her. As the sky got darker the place was lit by the bright red buds everyone was breathing on.

Varun took small polythene from his purse, took a bud of dried leaves, crushed it to powder with the tips of his fingers, mixed it with a little tobacco, and rolled the mix in a sheet into a cigarette-like thing, just like a professional cigarette maker, and lit it. Samantha's jaw dropped looking at his expertise. He sucked the rolled cigarette until it filled his lung capacity and released the smoke gradually. Within no time, his pupils floated in the red-nerved cloudy white background.

'This! This thing will get you out of all your troubles. I'm not sure if I can help you, but this will definitely do. LIFE SAVIOUR,' he said, lifting the rolled spliff like an Olympic torch. Samantha wondered how different it was from a cigarette. They both sat on the top of the tank in the cold breeze. She stayed in her own pleasant solitude staring at the passing sparkles of the vehicles from far away. She thought about one single thing that filled her heart: her brother.

Later that night, when Samantha reached home, she justified her delay by saying that she was with her new college friends. Her parents were pretty convinced and happy that she'd finally started getting along with other people.

CHAPTER 17

BANGALORE

3 Months Before

'Bunny!' Samantha ran to Simon and hugged him tightly. Her face was pressed to his chest, her panting synchronized with his heartbeat. 'Where were you so long? I was worried about you.'

'Hey buddy, relax. I just went on an office trip.' He caressed the top of her head and said, 'Look, I'm back now. I should've bet on who turns into a crybaby out of missing the other.' He laughed gracefully.

'I'm sorry. I'm sorry. I'm so sorry. I shouldn't have done that. I shouldn't have barged into your room. I shouldn't have put you in that race. I shouldn't have let you go. It's all my fault,' she cried.

'Wait. wait. Hold on. I'm here and I'm alright. I'm back to my little sister.'

She smiled with tears in her eyes and said, 'I can't believe it. I thought I'd lost you. Completely. I… I knew I had to bring you back, but I didn't know what to do or how to do it. I hated myself. I forgot how I used to live. I couldn't move, and neither could I move on. I never thought I could touch you like this.' She wiped the tears across her cheeks. 'That I could talk to you like this. Bunny, don't leave me again. Please.' She hugged him tighter than before with a weeping face. 'Take me along with you wherever you go.'

'Oh, kid. Where will I go without you?'

Samantha did not release Simon from her embrace. She found herself smiling after what felt like a lifetime. It seemed as if she felt happy for the first time since birth and teared up. Tears flickered to a spark when her fingers reached her face. She was thrown away from the hypnotic daydream. It made her realize how happy her life used to be. She felt surreal to have experienced the trance of meeting her brother again. The fact that it did not happen in real stabbed her inside.

She turned around from left to right, finding herself on the terrace, almost stoned amongst equally stoned men. It had been a little more than a couple of weeks since she was introduced to that place, and she was barely recognized as the opposite sex with her lean physique and loosely fitted clothes. The spliff in her hand burnt her fingers, waking her up from her favorite moment. She sucked on the cardboard filter and exhaled, cherishing the experience. Though her heart ached, she had a smile on her face remembering the hours spent hugging her brother. She had never experienced something like this in the past few months. She closed her eyes tight, uttering 'Come back. Come back. Come back. Don't go. Please come back.' Tears rolled across her cheeks.

'Dude...' Varun shook her by grabbing her shoulder as soon as he noticed her face turning pink and tears rolling onto her cheeks.

She recalled Varun's words from weeks prior. 'This stuff indeed does wonders.'

'I know right... I think our government needs to make use of this stuff. They can transform their work experience, you know, with new ideas implementing technology in agriculture, or to use innovative methods to grow food and not some freaking chemical bombs...'

'True that.' They both laughed together.

'Do you think everything is okay with Sam?' asked Mr. Victor.

'Of course.' Layla spoke confidently 'She is going to college, spending time with her friends. She is just not able to spend time with us, but that's okay. I'm happy she is on her own.'

Mr. Victor wanted to have a small chat with his daughter and went to her room. He knocked thrice at decent intervals. He pushed it slightly to check if the door was open and opened it finally. He did not find Samantha on her bed. He considered she might be in the restroom.

'Sam, it's me.' he said outside the door. 'Sorry to disturb you. I just wanted to have a chat. Anyway, I'll come later.' He suspected that something was wrong when there was no response. He went close to the restroom and happened to see the door unlocked. 'SAM?' he cried, rushing to the main door and found it locked as he did before getting to bed. After thoroughly checking the entire house, he realized the only way out was the back door and found it open.

Victor had already suspected that something was happening. He went back to Samantha's room to inspect. He found the college books still wrapped in tight polythene, he witnessed a wall full of photos in which Samantha and Simon were clicked together since childhood. Victor's heart melted looking at the pictures taken when Samantha was three months old, wrapped in a white cotton fabric and kept on Simon's lap. He took the picture off of the wall, revisiting the memories. The picture slipped onto an old shoe box which was camouflaged amongst other cardboard boxes filled with Simon's stuff. Victor picked the picture back up and doubted if the Adidas box was the one that he had gifted to Simon when he'd got his first job. The whole family knew that those shoes were one of Simon's favourites.

He slightly lifted the upper cover to be shocked at the sight. The box was full of a cigarette stash and buds. Victor could not believe his eyes and could not fathom what was happening. He collapsed on the bed for several minutes.

He ran to Mrs. Layla and cried, 'She is not alright, Layla.' His head shook in trauma. 'She is not alright, there is a box of cigarettes in her room,' he said with tears in his eyes.

'Cigarettes? Wha… What are you saying, Victor? I don't want to believe you.'

'I don't know.'

'Could be someone else's,' defended Layla with a ray of hope in her eyes.

'It could be. I don't know, and I don't even want to know. I do not want to hear anything bad about my daughter.'

'Victor, this is an unfortunate situation. Simon's loss has put us all on a rollercoaster. Imagine Samantha's situation. We need to be very careful and conscious about things happening. I think we need to give her some time to recover.'

CHAPTER 18

CHENNAI

'Shall we go to the meditation hall?' Neethu rushed Samantha an hour earlier than their regular time.

'Now?'

'Yes! Come on.'

'But Andrew is not here yet.'

'He's been stuck at the hospital since last night. He informed me that there is going to be another instructor at this time,' she answered, picking up the rolled yoga mat in one hand and a water bottle in the other. Neethu stood right at the entrance, as if she needed to run as soon the marathon whistle was blown, while Samantha didn't even recover from the news. 'Come, come. Fast,' she hurried.

Samantha slowly picked up her socks and dragged her legs to coordinate a walk. It was the first time Samantha was being taken out of that room without Andrew's presence, and she was hesitant about it. Both were uncomfortable about the new tutor and mostly about the meditating session without Andrew. Two middle-aged women came straight into the hall with yoga mats in their hands. Neethu and Samantha looked at each other's faces filled with shock. Another young man entered, who was then followed by a group of people dressed in workout clothes and carrying yoga mats.

'With other people?' Samantha was awed at the noisy crowd, as this was the first time she was put in a room to be a part of a big group of people. She felt it differently than the random crowd she saw at the exhibition, for she felt absolutely one amongst everybody in that room. Neethu immediately isolated herself outside of the meditation hall grabbing her phone. She came back to Samantha within a few seconds and said, 'Yes. It's with this batch.'

Samantha's eyes went bigger with mixed emotions. She was excited to see new people and also irritated with the noise they produced. She never knew that people from that locality used that hall for practicing meditation, for she was only taken after the whole crowd was gone. The people were silenced once the instructor arrived. Samantha felt relieved to be a part of the common crowd. She noticed the middle-aged women and small kids wearing white kurta pyjamas. The middle and old aged men. The meditation session resembled one of the activities at her school, which involved students from different grades. Samantha was glad that no gaze meant any different, there were no traces of compassion whatsoever. Everyone in the session sat on their mats equidistant from each other. They closed their eyes and practiced inhaling and exhaling by alternating the thumb and little finger of their right hand on their left and right nostrils. She was pleased by the coordination the entire group had.

'Can I go with this crowd every day?' Samantha asked Neethu with a twinkle in her eyes.

'Whatever the doctor says.'

She felt content but not complete. She subconsciously waited for Andrew. She wanted to tell him about her experience at the meditation session, she wanted him to know that being normal made her happy. She walked from the entrance to the balcony numerous times, rubbing her palms together. She sat in the reception area waiting for him.

Samantha's eyes followed through various footsteps that passed the entrance, waiting to spot Andrew's. She did not bother about the time, did not think of any work he could have had at the hospital, and did not realize that he actually was a full-time doctor in a hospital. It was an hour before she got back to her room. The nurse's phone buzzed when Samantha gave up and got up from her regular spot on the balcony facing the beach.

She did not think of that option till then, she had waited like a kid would wait for her father to arrive home after work. As soon as she heard the phone ring, she thought she could just call Andrew to converse. Her eyes widened at the idea; she asked the nurse to put Andrew on call.

Neethu thought about it for a second, gripped the phone, and shoved it back into her pockets. 'He should be on his way, why disturb him?'

Her response definitely spoiled Samantha's mood, her lips and eyes gone flat. Samantha could not take that response from the nurse. Without a second thought, she said 'I'm actually not feeling something inside, please can you tell him that I'm not well.' She kept her face drawn down with her moist eyes. The nurse, having no other choice, took her phone and dialled Andrew. The call was answered in four rings.

'All ok there?'

'Yeah. But–'

'Ok. I'm busy, I'll call you back,' said the firm voice and hung up. 'He is busy! Let's wait, he said he'll call back.' Her voice shivered. Samantha felt breathless not being able to connect with Andrew and was mad at him after the call. She could not digest the fact that she would not be seeing him at that moment.

'Busy?' Her ego insisted on the word to herself, frowned.

She sat on the couch with her mind full of thoughts. Since she started living in that dormitory her mornings were always filled with Andrew; he would come and wake her up most days, and sometimes he would wait until she rises up and then wish her a good day. She felt restless without Andrew's presence that day. She stared at the waves breaking into the shore; It seemed as if she had the power to control the sea. She quickly walked out, sliding into her flip-flops. She let herself sit on the steel chairs that were placed by the reception, waiting for the appearance of her favorite person. Neethu followed right behind when she left the room but went back, assured that Samantha would stay in the reception. Samantha noticed everything happening around her, she waited there until the watchman went into his room for lunch. As soon as he moved, she dived out within seconds without anyone noticing. She walked straight onto the road that led to the hospital. She was surprised by herself to have had the courage to step out of that dorm; Going to the hospital to meet Andrew was the only thought on her mind.

She walked briskly, halted every time there was a vehicle passing by or when she heard a loud honk. Patients leaving the dormitory without a doctor, nurse, or a family member was prohibited. Samantha had to walk straight for around 200 meters and cross a four-way main road in order to reach the hospital. She looked at the traffic signal and could not decide on which way to go. She followed an ambulance that was going towards the hospital entrance, crossing that road was indeed a task for her. She put a step forward and two backward as the vehicle passed by along with her. The same repeated for several minutes. She finally decided to run across the road irrespective of any vehicle crossing. She thought that would be the only possible way to cross this huge four-way lane.

Andrew clenched his jaw; he flinched every time the lady sat on the chair was triggered with an electric shock. This was the phase he would avoid for any patient to be put through. Andrew would suggest this only when the patients refused to talk to anyone, but only maunder to oneself. He mostly thought about Samantha though he was in treatment. Right after the treatment ended, he quickly steered his car to the dormitory. He saw a crowd gathered at the four-way junction. He jumped and peered from the car window. He hated his intuition as he pictured Samantha being the subject of the crowd, although he knew it was highly impossible. He got out of the car with trembling legs and ran towards the crowd.

'Excuse me. Please. Excuse.' He slowly squeezed himself through the dense crowd. He was startled to see Samantha.

'You came the wrong way, you idiot... Don't you know how to drive in a crossing?' screamed a person on a bike.

Andrew saw Samantha staring at the people yelling at each other. 'Samantha!' he screamed.

'Andrew!' She screamed back, her eyes going wide, accompanied by a broad smile. She was truly happy to find Andrew before reaching the hospital. A volcano erupted inside Andrew to see her out of the dormitory. Samantha went running across the crowd.

'Why are you here? Where is Neethu?' He frowned.

'Neethu doesn't know. I was coming to see you and this happened.' She pointed at the bikes in the centre of the crowd. Andrew clenched her hand, carefully passed through the wall of people, and reached the car across the traffic. Andrew's face was stiff, he couldn't show his anger on Samantha, and thus, stayed quiet.

'I did not tell Neethu that I was coming here. I wanted to see you. I knew you were busy, you just told me when she called. that's why..'

'I was in a freaking treatment. Damn it.' Andrew spoke louder than he usually would. 'Don't you understand what busy means? And don't you know that you shouldn't be coming out without anyone?' He kept his eyes on the road while he drove. Her eyes held up a rush of tears without spilling down. Her face turned almost red in embarrassment. She couldn't believe that she was yelled at by the person who treated her like a kid all this while. Both stayed quiet until they reached the dormitory.

'Watchman!' Andrew cried, his eyes fiercely searching for a security at the main gate. He walked hastily towards the front office; Samantha followed struggling to match his pace.

'He has gone for his lunch, Doctor. May I help you?' A worker rushed out from inside along with other staff and answered.

'How long? Since when was he gone?' Andrew was breathing hard while he spoke. Samantha literally felt heat waves from his body. 'So, when he goes for lunch will the gate be unattended? Who is to watch out for people entering or leaving the building?' His voice was unpleasant.

'Sorry sir, we will take care of that hereafter.' The staff mostly kept their eyes down to the ground but did not stop glancing at Samantha as a culprit. She did not like the way the staff looked at her. *Why are they looking at me like that? Do I look like a thief who tried to escape from jail?* She thought Andrew was overreacting in this situation.

'Tell him to meet me once he is back,' he said. They walked past the staff while their eyes persisted on Samantha. She was upset with Andrew's reaction to what she considered a simple act. Her eyes widened and face stiffened, she stayed motionless not knowing how to react. Andrew walked straight to Samantha's room. He raged upon the sight of Neethu with her phone.

'What is your job here?' His voice seemed to blow the roof away, his eyes turned to wine. Neethu, who partially abandoned herself in the world of the phone, was startled by dropping the phone down.

'Doc…doctor!' her words stumbled.

'What is your job apart from looking after Samantha? What were you doing when she was not around?' His eyebrow raised uncontrollably as he spoke.

'Doctor, she...she was in the reception waiting for you. So, I thought...'

'You thought? You cannot think, mam! You are not appointed to assume that she is here around. Your job is to look after her, be with her wherever she goes. Do you hear me? I don't think you understand what you're expected to do.'

'I know, Doctor. But she was just sitting in the reception.' Neethu's voice and hands shivered. Andrew held Samantha's hand and slowly took her to the balcony. The orangish tint in the sky reflected on both their faces, the cold breeze calmed Andrew a bit.

He spoke, 'Sam, I don't think you realize what a great risk it was to come out alone like that, without informing anybody. My God, I… I still can't believe you did that. That's a freaking stunt you have performed right now. This is not so fair from your side when we all are trying so hard to protect you and treat you. You have to be safe and this is the only place where you can be safe. Promise me you won't do it again!' said Andrew trying to catch her eye contact. Samantha avoided his sight as much as possible looking away into the sky. 'Sam!' Andrew called after a few moments. 'Sam, look at me.'

'You said I'm 21 now. Can I not decide if I want to come to see you or not? You need not react like I don't know what I'm doing.'

Her words melted him from all the chaos he had been facing since the previous night. An unstoppable smile appeared at the corner of his lips, 'Of course, you know what you're doing. All I want is for you to be safe. What if you weren't able to cross the road? What if some idiot drove recklessly? See, you are my responsibility.' He held her hands. Their gazes penetrated into each other's eyes. Samantha was captivated by the depth of his eyes. Her heart raced faster as she decrypted more than what he said, through his eyes. 'You are. Until you get back home. Okay? Please promise me now.' He waited for a response. She gave a slight nod with her eyes, and smiled from inside. He felt consent given for a lifetime.

Samantha sat at her usual place on the balcony filled with guilt and embarrassment. She waited until the residue of that moment evaporated. She felt at peace with whatever happened and realized the reason behind Andrew's rage. She was able enjoy fresh air from the balcony, birds chirping, and the sea laughing in joy. She knew that Neethu would also be going through the same and slowly walked up to her. She noticed her face all sunk in sadness.

'Would you like to get some coffee?' she asked the nurse politely.

'No. You help yourself please.'

'Are you okay?' Samantha slowly approached.

'I'm alright.'

'No. You're not.'

'I don't have anything to tell you, Samantha. Who in the world cares if I'm upset.'

'Don't say that. I do.' She placed her hand on Neethu's in a comforting manner.

'Then you shouldn't have gone outside. And he shouldn't have shouted at me without even listening to what I was saying.'

Samantha's eyes widened realizing she was the reason behind her being upset. 'Oh, no. Neethu, I'm so sorry.'

'I understand that he cares for you, he doesn't want a thing to happen to you. But I'm a normal person with normal work expectations. I should be allowed to make mistakes, sometimes.' Neethu flumped on the couch, pinching the bridge of her nose. Though she felt sorry for what Neethu had faced, her words describing the way Andrew cared for her delighted Samantha. Her heart flew in the air, and her eyes smiled and cheeks shied away.

That evening, Samantha woke up from an extended nap to a package that was kept right next to her. The package looked like a brick wrapped with a black polka-dotted sheet. Her hands spontaneously picked up the pack without any guess. She looked around. 'Neethu,' she called with her broken sleepy voice. She heard an answer from far away, and she wondered if she actually heard it or if it was just her hallucination. She waited, inspecting the package by twisting it all around until Neethu showed up. *Don't touch others' stuff.* She heard her mother's voice in the back of her head.

'Hey...' Neethu entered the room with a smirk at the corner of her lips.

'Is this yours?' Samantha pointed at the pretty package.

'No, that's for you! Doctor asked me to give it to you once you're up,' she said with a stiff face.

'Andrew? What's in it?' Samantha's eyes twinkled. She ripped apart the packaging as soon as she knew it belonged to her.

'I don't know,' Neethu shrugged casually.

Samantha's curiosity peaked. The package revealed itself to be a white hard box with huge text which read 'Samsung Note'. Samantha jumped with surprise; her lips were drawn into a broad smile. 'A phone? for me?' She opened the cover wrapped around unveiling a bluish metallic surfaced phone with the longest screen she had ever seen. Her hands shivered, holding something which felt premium. She still could not fathom the reason behind being gifted with a phone.

Samantha spent the rest of the day in bed, exploring the new phone. She scrolled the menu screens, impressed by the buttery smooth interface. She could not stop admiring the classily laid qwerty keypad. She only remembered borrowing her father's phone to type on a

T9 keypad making random beeping noises. She opened the messages, with the tip of her thumb typed her name by touching the letters one by one gently. She zoomed the camera into the sea and clicked multiple shots, joying at the radiant colours captured. She was amazed by the replica a gadget was capable of delivering.

'Do you like it?' She heard the voice she was waiting for from behind while she was still struggling to click a perfect picture.

'Andrew... hi.' She looked charmed.

'Hello. Someone looks happy.' He approached slowly.

She threw a narrow look. 'But why?'

'Well, to communicate. You can call your parents or me whenever you want to. In any situation, drop me a text and I'll call you back. Okay?'

'Really? Can I call my parents?'

'I've saved all the contacts in it. Your parents', Neethu's, and mine.' Samantha giggled and looked at him with shinier eyes. It wasn't the phone that mattered to her, it was how quickly her need was addressed and fixed. Although Andrew was relieved to see her happy, her impulsiveness haunted him. On hindsight, he realized that this has been one of the core behaviours of Samantha.

CHAPTER 19

3 Months Before

Samantha rang the calling bell of her home after dusk. Layla opened the door with a weird look on her face. Her look made Samantha uncomfortable.

'Yes?' she said while she walked past Layla, prompting for whatever her mother wanted to say.

'How was college today?'

'It was alright. Actually boring,' she spontaneously said, thinking about entire of the week that she spent with Varun in the empty concrete tank, smoking up, skipping college.

'Are you sure?' asked Layla firmly, sitting next to Samantha.

'Yeah. Why?'

She shrugged. 'I got a call from your college.'

Samantha's heart raced with Layla's words. Her forehead sweated within seconds. She looked at Layla, her eyes filled with guilt.

'About your absence,' Layla stressed.

Samantha slowly walked past Layla. Layla held Samantha's arm at the elbow and spoke, 'What's happening Sam? Where have you been if not to the college?'

'I will go to the college tomorrow.'

'My question was not that.'

Samantha tried and release her hand from her mother's grip. 'Ma, I was safe. You don't need to worry about me.' Her face warmed up with the rapid rush of blood when she back-answered her mother. She walked straight to her room, escaping her mother's deathly stare.

Samantha sat on the bed grinding her teeth in nervousness, her palms were almost wet. The door of her room opened within a couple of minutes.

'It is better you stay home for a few days. I'll inform the college about your absence,' said her mother's sternest voice followed by a slam of the door.

Samantha felt that she was being pushed into a pit of darkness, far away from her one little space of joy in this world currently. She aggressively ripped open the zip of her bag, dug into all the compartments in search of a cigarette or a pot, and found nothing. She imagined herself sulking in the room, deprived of everything she would possibly need in order to get her brother's memories back. She jumped off the bed, ran across, and searched the entire room, inside out at all the regular places where she would hide cigarettes. She needed one, at least one cigarette at that moment to recover from breathlessness.

She fell on her knees, pulling her hair almost out of her scalp. She grew fearful as time passed. Fear of forgetting. Fear of not being able to remember even the tiniest details about Simon, fear of getting back to normal. The feeling of fear threatened her, made her feel extremely vulnerable. She knew that this was the worst moment of her life and felt worthless. Samantha wept, she then clenched her neck with her two palms and squeezed as hard as possible. She released when she coughed her eyes out.

She ran to the balcony hoping to breathe; the cold breeze hit her face but did not help in the way she felt. Her eyes focused and stayed still on to the huge concrete water tank. Thoughts rushed into her head effortlessly, which she was consciously avoiding all this while. *If this is going to be the situation, then I cannot be in this world.* She quietly snuck out of her room to find none in the living room. She was wretched when she found both the front and back doors locked. Samantha became furious knowing the door were locked purposefully. She led herself quickly into the kitchen, searching for a knife. The kitchen was right next to her parent's room where Victor had already sensed something odd happening. Samantha opened the chamber right below the stove and moved all the spoons noisily trying to find a knife. She then opened the next cabinet, where she found all kinds of spatulas. After exhausting the little patience she had, she looked around the open space on the counter and found the bread and butter knife in a dark brown wooden jar. Samantha, who knew that the butter knife would do a no-good job of taking a life, took the bread knife fiercely, making the jar roll on to the opposite side. She looked at the textured edge of the knife for a brief moment and took a deep breath.

'Sam?' her father cried. 'What are you—' he stepped forward.

'Don't come. Don't you dare to come near me.'

Layla hurriedly approached Victor, unable to believe what she was looking at with her naked eyes. 'Darling, give that to me. What are you doing?'

'I said don't come closer.' Samantha spoke with a shivered voice.

'Look. Let's sit and talk,' Victor spoke gently.

'Enough!' she cried, 'I don't want to be here. You guys think I'm the reason Simon died. And you all pretend to be nice to me. I don't want this. I'm leaving.'

'What? What makes you say that? Sam, please listen to me. Come to Mumma. We never thought that about you.' Layla walked forward.

'You do. You do.'

Before Layla took her second step, Samantha sawed her left hand with irregular pressure or motion which created deep injury, her skin ripped like a paper that is pierced and dragged recklessly.

She endured the pain with a cry. 'Maa' Samantha cried her guts out. She collapsed there in the kitchen, sopping her own blood.

CHAPTER 20

Good night. You can ping me here anytime.

Samantha received a WhatsApp message after an hour of struggling with whether or not to call Andrew. She jumped looking at the message, her heart beating fast. She was all brightened up. Her fingers trembled not knowing how to respond.

Hi. She bit her nails staring at the screen for a response.

Hi. Still up?

Butterflies flew starting from her stomach and reaching her heart, giving her goosebumps. She looked at the top right corner of the screen to realize it was half past ten. 'Damn,' she said under her breath. She sat on the bed with her back resting on the headboard. She had covered herself cosily with the quilt. After a deep thought, she replied.

I was trying to sleep.

Oops. sorry if I disturbed you. Good night!

No, wait.

Yes. I'm right here. His words made her feel he was right beside her.

Are you busy?

Not at all. What's up?

Just wanted to say... thank you! I shouldn't have said that this is a jail. I'm sorry for my words the other day.

Why, no silly. As I already told you, it's my responsibility. I love doing this to you. I understand where those words came from, and I'm happy that you got out of jail (kidding) :-p

Her heart melted. She smiled at his wittiness in silence. Both stared into the light focused on their faces expecting a message from the other but not knowing how to continue the conversation. Her eyes flashed looking at the 'typing...' prompt on the screen.

Shall we get to bed?

Sure! she replied with a bit of disappointment.

Good night, Sam. Sleep tight.

Good night.

She tried to zoom in on the tiny display picture and jerked in surprise when it popped out to fit the screen. She zoomed furthermore, noticing an unusual attire; he was standing at the peak of some mountain in a red

T-shirt and cargo pants. She admired the way he stood, posed, and smiled.

Didn't sleep yet?

Her fingers froze for a second as if caught by a teacher doing something mischievous.

How did you know??? she asked, genuinely surprised.

Haha. it would show 'Online' under your name if you're using the App. I'm sure it's 'online' under my name too. That is how.

'Oops,' she said under her breath and replied. **Yea it is. To be honest, I'm not sleepy at all.**

It should be because of the new device. No problem, explore a bit and get to sleep. Don't make it too late.

Maybe. Hey, are you sleepy? Samantha felt more courageous to chat rather than to talk in person.

Not really. But I have a special power!

Really! What is it?

I can sleep the moment I close my eyes.

Samantha giggled in silence; all her teeth shone in the phone light. **Impressive.**

Thank you :-)

But, could you hold on for just ten minutes before closing your eyes? :-p

Sure. Why not.

Thank you. Actually, the other day you told me about the first time you saw me. What about after that? Did you see me again?

Of course, I did. Every Sunday in the church. You were regular to the choir. Spoke to almost everyone jovially. Most of the time I used to skip church due to my rotational shifts at the hospital. I was able to see you otherwise.

Samantha's eyes shone reading that message from Andrew. She imagined everything in her little imaginary cloud, her crossing hands and praying, singing beautifully and harmonizing with others, and wishing the elders cheerfully.

Oh, I almost forgot. There used to be a stray dog nearby the church, it was pure black and had grey eyes. You always made sure you fed him while leaving and he also would follow you. No idea how far, but he did.

Samantha smiled at her own generosity which made her heart happy. **Crazy!** she replied.

Andrew meanwhile gave a brief thought to telling her anything more than that about her past. He for sure knew that it would not be a good idea.

Yeah, right?

Okay. Thank you so much for sharing this. It made my day! I guess you can close your eyes now. I shall too.

Great. No problem. Sleep well. Good night.

Good night!

She closed her eyes with a constant smile on her face, speculating more other things she could've done in the church. And for the very first time in that dorm, she felt self-love.

CHAPTER 21

Samantha rose with a wide smile. Her cheeks bore a pinkish tint naturally. Her eyes carried the spark no matter what she did. She had an energy that could power up anyone she came across, practiced yoga effortlessly, with utmost joy. Unlike any other day, that day she had already decided what to wear. She opened the wardrobe and very delicately took the yellow kurta that Andrew had purchased along with the casual clothes.

Right from day one since she was admitted to the dormitory, she had never thought of her clothing. She just went with what was available at that moment. Samantha did not bother to wear the kurta even when Andrew took her to the theme park. She felt that it was all for good reason that she did not opt to wear it till that day, though she liked it. She got ready as quickly as possible. She kept smiling throughout her shower. She looked at the clock crossing at 8.40 a.m. *He will be here anytime now. Oh my god.* She walked up and down the hall, biting her nails.

'Are you okay?' Neethu interrupted her march.

'Yes! Absolutely.'

'Shall I bring breakfast for you?'

'No. I… I'm not hungry actually.' Her stomach rumbled as she spoke.

'Well, I'm not sure if the doctor will buy that answer.'

'Okay,' she sighed. 'I'll get it by myself. I'll head to the canteen.'

'Good. By the way, you look pretty.'

Samantha grinned. She headed towards the canteen and wished everyone a very good morning; everyone wished her back, cheered with her energy, surprised. When the clock struck 9 am, Samantha was there in her dormitory, finished practicing yoga and having her breakfast. She expected Andrew to be there at any minute and at that moment, she realized she had not figured one thing out yet. *How am I going to tell him?*

Her eyes widened without affecting the wide smile. She walked several times around her bed making a semicircle, trying to collect ideas on how to express love. All at once, her palms sweated, her head swirled, and also fretted, at the thought of looking at the person who made her more comfortable in recent times. She took her mobile, clicked on the colourful browser icon, and typed 'How to propose to Andrew'. She paused and giggled at her own stupidity, removed 'Andrew' and replaced it with 'a man'. The king of web searches threw numerous options at Samantha to her surprise. Pictures of a woman kneeling down on one leg in front of a guy, a red pillow that read 'I love you' on it, and a blog post titled 'How to Propose a Man: Top 10 Steps' lined up on the top bar. Multiple blog posts on how to make a move while proposing to a guy lined up consequently.

Samantha's head rolled away looking at all the crazy options the web page had suggested. She convinced herself that all those ideas took a long time to plan and flipped her mobile on the bed carelessly. She decided to go with the flow. She recalled the chanting for Pranayam. She sat at the edge of her bed, her eyes closed, inhaled and exhaled gradually with Andrew's face in her mind's eye with every breath she took. She opened her eyes after calming herself down. She glanced at the clock and found it was six minutes past 10 a.m. *Andrew should've been here by now.* She peered at the entrance. *What happened? Where is he*? The wide smile on her face faded as time passed.

It's 11 a.m., and Andrew hasn't shown up yet. Samantha opened her WhatsApp chat with Andrew and stared at the screen to check if he was online. The space below his name did not flash. She thought of sending a nice proposal picture to Andrew but thought that could be lame and kiddish, moreover, she was certain she wanted to look at his face while expressing her love. She ended up sending 'Hi'. She stared at the double tick next to her message to turn blue; they did not seem to change colour. She gripped her mobile tight with anxiety.

She jerked when it vibrated and immediately unlocked it to find a promotional message from the network provider. She tutted, throwing the mobile on the mattress. Around twenty-five minutes later, Andrew responded. 'An emergency case, will text later.'

Samantha had texted Andrew the previous night to get to know about his arrival at the dormitory. According to her, Andrew was already one and a half hours late, and on top of that, his message about texting later took a ride on her temper. She took deep breaths, counted numbers, and tried to divert her thoughts to anything other than Andrew. She had been practicing meditation hard, in order to keep her anxiety in check, but at that moment she almost forgot all she had learned. Having spent most of the day trying to avoid thoughts about Andrew, she was surprised that she was only thinking more and more about the man she loved every fleeting minute.

It was a few minutes past 4 p.m. and Samantha had not moved from the wooden chair on the balcony, rather had spent thinking about all the life happenings with Andrew in the future. Her thoughts kept her happy. After a while, she had drained her patience and wanted to meet him right away. She was also considerate for the situation not to turn out like the last time when the security, the caretaker, the receptionist, and herself were blasted by Andrew back-to-back. *The hospital is just five minutes away, what could happen? I am totally fine. Why should I think so much about just getting down, crossing the four-lane, walking a few minutes, reaching the hospital, and meeting Andrew? See, that sounds simple.*

She drew a map in her head and motivated herself. She took her mobile in hand, slid her flip-flops on, and bolted down the stairs toward the entrance. She felt parched due to the fast since her breakfast, without even a sip of water. She headed towards the water dispenser in the reception. She clicked the 'Cold' button thrice, realizing there was no water, she then moved the cup under 'Normal', which dispensed a few more drops, and she peered into the water can with a frown. The dispenser could barely fill the paper cup.

She involuntarily dragged herself towards the canteen in search of another water dispenser, where she was thunderstruck. She was paralyzed for a moment, encountering Andrew. She felt a bit of her heart wreck to see him sitting with another woman. The sight seemed surreal which she had never anticipated. His V-shaped torso and the back of his head were the least needed for her to make out that it was him. She slowly moved towards the water dispenser but could not take her eyes off the woman he was sitting with. She studied the woman and thought, *A lady, whose hair is longer and smoother than mine, whose skin is clearer than mine, who is prettier than me*. She saw the anonymous woman touch Andrew's wrist across the table.

Samantha gasped and said to herself, 'A lady who can touch him.' She gulped the water from the paper cup and threw the half-crushed cup into the trash bin from a distance of three feet. She headed back swiftly in order to escape from Andrew's sight. The crushed cup missed the mouth of the bin and fell on the floor right next to it, making a noise in the quiet place. Andrew, along with the woman sitting with him, and the guy on the kitchen counter all turned to the unusual noise. Samantha saw everyone's eyes turn from the paper cup to herself within seconds. 'Oh, no,' she mumbled, putting a smile mixed with guilt on her face while she picked up the cup and threw it into the bin correctly.

'Hey, Sam.' Andrew waved at her spontaneously. Samantha, having no other choice, dragged herself slowly towards him. She kept looking at the floor while walking to not meet their eyes.

'Shreya, this is Samantha. I said..'

'Yea, S... Samantha! I've heard a lot about you. How are you?' She spoke gracefully with her eyebrows raised. Samantha stared at her long and neatly done manicure.

She nodded irregularly. 'I should actually be going, the…the nurse is waiting upstairs,' Samantha stuttered, not being able to accompany them even a moment more.

'Oh, okay, you go, I'll come in a while.' Andrew's tone was more casual than usual. Samantha left the place walking briskly with a firm face and tight lips.

'Is she okay?' Shreya did not take her eyes off Samantha until she passed out of her sight.

Samantha locked herself in the restroom and sobbed. She did not know exactly why she was crying. She definitely felt pain. She could not look at Andrew being close to a woman who seemed superior to her in every way possible. The image ran through her head over and again causing more pain. She wiped her tears as soon as she heard Andrew's voice and rushed out of the bathroom with damp eyes. She walked around him still avoiding eye contact.

'What's wrong? Where is Neethu?' he asked, looking around.

'No, nothing. Just temperature.' Her tone was low; she felt small at that moment.

'Temperature?' Andrew pressed the back of his palm against her forehead. Her heart shattered into pieces as soon as she felt the touch of his hand. *The hand she touched.* She moved her head away from his palm in disgust.

'Hey, lemme check.'

'I'm okay now!'

'Oh. Okay then.'

'I thought you were busy with a patient,' Samantha said, looking at the sea from the edge of the balcony while the cold wind blew on her face.

'Yes, I was. And I saw Shreya waiting for me in my office. One hour had just passed within a snap.' He smiled as he spoke. *One hour!* She frowned. *And I was waiting for you here like a puppy waiting for her owner.* She ground her teeth.

'You know, Shreya is also a doctor. We studied together.' His voice expressed explicit nostalgia.

'Oh! You never mentioned her before?' Her voice could not conceal jealousy.

'Uh, she... We lost touch.' His words stumbled. 'I mean, nothing to hide from you. She was my ex-girlfriend. We broke up two years ago.' He shrugged.

Samantha breathed harder. She felt blood rush to her face knowing that the anonymous woman was no longer anonymous, but a person closer than a friend. 'She was your girlfriend?' she asked in shock.

'Yea, she was. It was in college.' He spoke in a convincing tone.

'So, now you're friends again?' she finally looked at Andrew and asked genuinely.

'Well, not really.'

'What do you mean?'

Andrew for a second regretted sharing this information with Samantha at that point in time but thought that she had to know anyway. 'She wants to get back together. She says she'll make it work this time.' He spoke carelessly, adjusting the rolled sleeves of his shirt. Samantha felt her whole body turning into a kiln. She faced the beach again not to make her feelings obvious. She clenched the metal pole of the balcony and took a deep breath.

'Leave her, you said you wanted to talk. What's the matter?' he asked.

'Nothing! actually, I'm not keeping well. I want to sleep now. You… carry on. you must be busy.' Her broken voice bore pain.

'Is it? Wait, I'll—'

'No! Thank you. I just want to sleep.'

'Are you sure? Because…'

'Very sure!' she said firmly.

'Okay, you get some sleep. I'll be around if you need me. I'm done with my work at the hospital.'

'Okay.' She gasped, revealing the bones of her throat as soon as Andrew left the room. She could not think straight. *So, you'll just carry on with her, right? After all, we're just a doctor and a patient*, she thought to herself and smirked. *How stupid of me. How could I… could've thought about proposing to him. He is my doctor after all.* Samantha paused, shifting her eyes from left to right rapidly. Tears rolled as her heart wrenched in pain. "But I love him. I can't stop thinking about a future with him." She cried, her face pushed against the pillow. She could not think beyond Andrew. She fell fast asleep before she could make peace with it.

CHAPTER 22

Andrew was on his way to the dormitory when he received a call from Victor. He pulled over by a bus stop looking at his phone with a million questions. Victor's call was the last thing he had expected at nine a.m. 'Hi, sir!' He consciously kept his voice firm.

'Hey, Andrew. How are you?' Victor dragged his words.

'I am all okay, sir. Sam is also doing well.'

'Yes, that is what I called about.' Andrew frowned; his eyelids narrowed as he listened carefully. 'I think Samantha can cope hereafter. I am planning to head over tonight and will reach the hospital early tomorrow to bring her back home.' It took a moment for Andrew to comprehend Victor's words.

'Hello?' Victor checked after not receiving a response from the other end.

'Yes, sir. Sure. okay.'

'Okay, take care. bye.'

Andrew looked in the distance with thoughts filling his mind. *What? What happened; what did he mean by she will cope hereafter? I... I'm lost.* He left his body in the support of his car's bonnet and stayed there for several minutes, lost in thought. Once he got back to reality, he raced to the dormitory to make sure Samantha was alright.

Andrew waited outside the glass door which led to the open meditation area surrounded by potted plants. He stood there with his arms crossed, staring at Samantha through the glass.

She sat facing the west from the entrance. She felt the urge to turn and look at the entrance but refrained. Samantha had almost learned the art to meditate without a break in concentration. She sat on her yoga mat with her eyes closed, occupying only one-fourth of the portion at the center. She focused on the point between her eyebrows, taking regular and long breaths. She placed her concentration on the sound of waves, which were faintly mixed with the other noises around her. She gathered her immense concentration towards the waves. Her body weighed as light as a feather. She was surprised at how miraculously capable a human body was by the clear sound of waves. Meditation had been helping her in coming to terms with her brother's absence in her life. She could sense a skin, deep inside her and happy with the memories. She would sit in meditation for hours and feel close to her brother with all her heart; she no longer cribbed about the physical presence. Samantha slowly opened her eyes with the contentment of communicating with the waves far away. She felt an urge to look at the entrance. She quickly turned and was shaken by the uninterrupted gaze of Andrew. She did not smile, not wish or wave, she immediately turned back pretending to search for the bird she was listening to.

Andrew felt strange waves from Samantha's behaviour. She had never treated him that way. He knocked on the glass door twice. He waved when Samantha turned to the knock. She nodded, conveying that she had already noticed him there. They both took the stairs and descended in silence. Andrew did not know how to convey the message of her dad's call.

'Sam!' Andrew broke the silence when they reached the entrance of her room. She turned towards him without meeting his eyes. 'Sam, your dad called. He said… he is coming tonight to—'

'I know. I called him this morning and asked him to take me home.' Although she felt the utmost heat waves between them, she did not look into his eyes.

He was frozen for a few moments, unable to believe her words. 'Why? I mean, you still need to be here until your memory is back. There might be a lot of complications if there is a rush of memory. That's a lot for you to handle. You, you know what I mean?'

'No. It's ok, doctor. I think I can handle it.' She shrugged, looking at him. She walked past him into the dormitory, avoiding any further conversation. Her words hit hard on Andrew. He felt a nail pierce into his heart. He remained at the entrance, cluelessly leaning against the wall. Her words ran through his mind once again, one word at a time. 'Doctor?' he repeated. She had never addressed Andrew as 'doctor', rather he never preferred so.

Andrew waited in the living room to have a conversation with Samantha. He wanted to know why she had suddenly decided to leave home from the healing process. Why? What's wrong? Did something bother you? Or did someone hurt you in any way? Andrew wanted to ask all the questions at once as soon as he saw her coming out of the room. Instead, he waited for her to settle and spoke with a consciously calm voice, 'May I ask, why?'

'Sorry, what?' she acted puzzled, though she knew what he was referring to.

'Sam! Please tell me why you have decided to go home without completing your treatment.' She stared at the floor, grinding her teeth. 'What is bothering you? Tell me, perhaps I can fix it. Trust me,' he promised.

'There is nothing to fix, doctor. And that is why I'm going. I think I'm alright.'

'Where is this 'doctor' coming from? Guess many things have changed overnight, haven't they? Look, I sincerely apologize to you if there is anything wrong that happened without my knowledge.'

'NO! There is nothing wrong with you. I miss my parents, I miss my family. I want to go.' She looked into his eyes. Her eyes bore a lot of pain, which she would like to conceal. Andrew felt her pain as his own. He did not speak a word nor ask a question after that.

'I don't have any business in this place without you. I brought you here, I shall take you back. Let's leave tomorrow,' he said after giving a fierce thought to it. Samantha agreed in silence.

Andrew was ready in his car the next morning. He kept a pair of sunglasses, sunscreen, jerkin, soft drinks, and a few magazines ready for Samantha. He had a war going on in his head with a ton of unanswered questions, which he had satiated with her one response on missing her family which had him only care more for her; he knew the pain of missing one's own family. He has been enduring that pain since he was sixteen and had always thought that no one in this world, even his worst enemies, should face it. Andrew had his struggles in his life. He lost his parents at sixteen, after which he had lived with his maternal grandparents. He lost his grandparents when he was 28, a year ago before he met Samantha.

Samantha took leave of the place she had been reborn at. Everyone in the dormitory who knew her, the nurses, the canteen people, and the watchman, gave their decent farewell. She had grown a lifetime of memories from this place. She had learned the most important lesson in her life, to grieve. Samantha had been struggling with this since her childhood. Though she only remembered a glimpse of her early age, she was told by her parents that when she had lost her puppy, she kept crying for almost a month, did not go to school, and they struggled to make her eat. She had not improved a bit since then and had a similar experience when she lost her brother. Now, Samantha knew how to handle loss; rather, she knew how to let herself grieve.

Samantha did not miss noticing each tree, post, or bird that passed by. While her eyes shuffled from one tree to another, she remembered every event that happened after she found herself for the first time in the dormitory. She recalled how she hated that place at first, and how it had turned into an untold home. She remembered looking at Andrew as a stranger, and now, all she could think about was him. She thought about how simple and silly life was to get attached or adapted to things that were alien at first. She wondered how her life would be after getting back home. She doubted how she would interact with her parents after a break of what felt like a lifetime to her. Her thoughts went deeper than the forest that surrounded the highway they were driving through.

CHAPTER 23

'The weather is nice, isn't it?' Andrew's voice pulled Samantha back to reality. She nodded, rolling her eyes to the sky through the mirror she was leaning on. 'You know what? It's weird I didn't mention this to you till now, but this drive drags me back to that day when we both came to Chennai. I put you in an ambulance with emergency medication and followed you right behind.' She gasped, and he continued, 'I did not dare to take my eyes off the back window of that ambulance even for a moment.' He paused and sighed. 'It feels like yesterday. I cannot believe we are going back already. I'm glad you're fine and ready to start a new life. You'll do great, Sam, I strongly believe so.'

Only then it occurred to Samantha, something she had never thought of since the day she was brought to the dormitory. Andrew was in Chennai with her, but that was not his place. He was constantly taking care of her, but that was not his full-time job. He was at service for Samantha no matter what. She recalled her mother telling her that she was taken to a different city for treatment, *but according to Andrew's words I was brought here the same night BECAUSE of the accident.* 'Why… was I brought to Chennai?' The words rolled out of Samantha's mouth right after the thought struck her mind.

'Huh?' Andrew's eyes widened.

'Why wasn't I hospitalized in Bangalore? And why did you come along with the ambulance? Why?'

Andrew kept staring at the road while he decided whether or not to respond to her questions. 'Well..." He cleared his throat. She notice his knuckles were pale as he gripped the steering wheel. 'I thought I needn't tell you this, but I think it's time. I told you about my mom, remember?'

'Yes.'

'She died due to depression.'

Samantha's jaw dropped, and her eyes took a straight turn to his face. 'I'm sorry.'

'No, it's okay. After the loss of my dad, my mother was clearly struggling to cope with it. Although, she did not give any symptoms till the end. Especially when she was with me. She never spoke to me about dad, and she tried to be as normal as possible around me. But my grandparents told me that she wasn't herself when I left for school. She slept all day and seldom ate. Later on, only at the very end did they understand that she was depressed. She denied talking to anyone, even to me. She stopped eating the little she used to eat along with me. She would scream if someone forced her. Dad's loss did hurt me, I think Mom compensated for it. I was young enough to be able to get along with my life. But Mom…'

He sighed. 'We could've saved her only if someone had noticed her at the early stages. She is the reason I became a psychiatrist. I... I think it's very cruel of our families and self-centred societies to not give attention to a soul which is slowly burning itself. From then on, I promised myself that I would pay attention to people's emotions around me and I wouldn't allow anyone, literally anyone out of my power to have a death like my mother's. I have hosted lots of seminars explaining various symptoms of this. When I saw you, I felt that you were almost in a similar situation after Simon's loss.' Her head turned towards him automatically in shock. 'Your parents also noticed the symptoms, and I volunteered to help you. I was certain not to let you endure that. Why Chennai… because you never wanted to be admitted to a hospital. We tried admitting you to a hospital a couple of times and failed. As soon as you would wake up and realize it was the hospital, you would turn fierce and throw things at people. Out of my search, Chennai is the only place that had this kind of hospital. You… You were in a home-like dormitory for a reason, Sam.'

Samantha did not look away or blink until Andrew finished talking. His answers gave her a new perspective to look at him. The respect she had for Andrew only grew more. 'Stop. Can you stop the car please?' She choked on the lump of pain that formed in her throat.

'Sure. Are you okay?' He immediately pulled over in the middle of a never-ending highway, behind them a vastly spread forest they had just passed. Samantha got out, feeling suffocated inside. She gasped, walking away from the car. She gestured to Andrew not to come any closer, and he obeyed. She cried her guts out. She knew she needed to vent for several reasons; for what her parents and Andrew were put to go through; for what Andrew's mother had gone through; and most importantly, for tomorrow, when she would have to deal without Andrew.

The greenery she had witnessed at that moment somehow made her nostalgic. She was happy and grateful to have been protected by Andrew. Her mind revised all the moments in retrospect since she woke up in the dormitory, and she thought that everything Andrew did was possibly the right thing. *After all*, she smirked, *anybody should have the freedom to choose their loved ones. Just the way I chose him, he can choose Shreya. Yea... he can choose anyone he wants.* She turned to Andrew with utmost regret for spoiling her own journey with the most precious man. Andrew waited in the car until she took enough time as she wanted and handed over a bottle of water and tissues when he thought it was okay to barge in.

After an unexpected deep conversation, Andrew and Samantha continued their journey mostly in silence. They were in silence but not their minds weren't. 'I'm sorry if anything I said earlier worried you. That's the last thing I ever want to happen,' Andrew said.

'No. not your fault.' She did not turn away from the window.

'Okay.'

'I think you can stop worrying about me. You've already wasted much of your time.'

'Never.' Andrew tried to catch her eyes and added, 'Silly. Never say that. I've never treated you anything less than myself. Never have I ever thought you were just a patient.'

'Yeah.' She thought, *it could've been better if I were treated just as a patient.*

The toughest thing in this world is when you have extreme love and not be able to show it.

Samantha sensed the depth of his thoughts in his eyes, the tension was just there in the air around them. 'Do you wanna say anything?'

'No.' He shook his head vigorously. *I would've. If only I could say those three words to you, without this baggage around us. Why not freedom of expressing love as simple as expressing likeness? Is it because of the commitment it carries? Why does it even have to be two ways?* He wished he could say it louder to her.

She blinked tight, remembering the disturbing sight of him with Shreya. She relaxed her eyes and chanted internally, *let go. Let go... Yes, you have never treated me like a patient. But the maximum you could do was consider me a friend, rather than a close one,* she thought. Out loud she said, 'I know, Andy. I didn't mean to hurt you.' She looked at him and said, 'Thank you! Thank you for everything you did. It means nothing less than a new life for me.'

Andrew was happy Samantha had gone back to calling him Andy as she always had. 'It was my absolute pleasure helping you cope with the situation, Sam. I did not do anything more.'

Andrew had pulled over at a fancy restaurant on the highway for lunch. He had searched for places early in the morning before they could start and had fixed this after reviewing all the comments and ratings. The place had a homely setup with authentic wooden furniture, and black-inked portraits of women, birds, and animals hung on the wall. A warm yellow light was suspended at the centre of the table. They both were seated at a small square table attached to the window, covered with cream curtains allowing minimal sunlight. Samantha was seated comfortably in a cushioned chair admiring the paintings around her. The place boosted her mood with a wave of joy. An order was placed: a spicy red sauce spaghetti for Samantha, a white sauce pasta for Andrew, and a grilled chicken.

'Over the time I spent in Chennai, I learned to make nice chicken gravy from my cook. I'll make it for you one day,' Andrew said.

'Actually,' Samantha said, stirring the pasta, 'do you think we'll meet again? I mean, once we're home, you may get quite busy with your life. Right?'

'What makes you think that we wouldn't meet?' Andrew asked, slowly swirling the spaghetti with his fork.

'To be honest, now that you guys are back together, you may get married, right?' Samantha winked, showing no trace of her disappointment.

'Wha... what?' Hhe frowned, dropping the fork on the chinaware plate, making noise. His heart raced thinking Samantha was referring to his love for her.

'Yeah. Your ex-girlfriend has come back, you were blu...' She paused when the waiter interrupted to ask about dessert. They declined, and she waited for him to leave before she continued. 'Sorry. Now that your ex-girlfriend has come back; you were also blushing the other day. So, I guessed...'

'Oh my god, you gave me a heart attack!' Andrew relaxed his stiffened body. 'C'mon, Shreya came back, yes.' Andrew held the chicken meat with the fork and ran through it with the knife while he spoke. 'But it's not like I still love her. Once gone is gone. I don't believe in patch-ups; once love dies in a person, it remains dead. Wow, amazing chicken,' he said, having had his first bite.'

'But, you said...' She paused and thought for a moment, gazing over one of the lights on her right.

'You said she wants to get back together? And that you guys would make it work this time?' Samantha eagerly waited for Andrew's response.

'What? Uh... yeah, those were her words. She wanted to get back together. She promised she would make it work this time. But I cannot, Sam. I just cannot turn the switch on when she wants and off when she doesn't. I have given my hundred percent when I was in love with her, it did not suffice. Well, it's over, we cannot redo a few things in life, and love tops that list, at least for me.' Andrew shrugged.

'Oh.' Samantha took a deep sigh of relief. She slipped a smile of triumph at the corner of her lips and refrained immediately. She cursed herself under her breath. Andrew noticed her unusual behaviour after their conversation. 'Excuse me!' Samantha went to the hand-washing area and pretended to wash her hands. She looked at her reflection in the mirror and allowed the irresistible grin to grow. Her eyes twinkled with joy. She pinched the bridge of her nose and smiled. 'Stupid, stupid, how stupid am I.' She took a deep breath, 'Gosh, what do I do now?' she said while exhaling.

She got back to the table and pulled a tissue from the tissue holder, letting it swing a couple of times. She took the fork from the pasta bowl, dipped it in the semi-dried sauce from the side of the bowl, and slowly stained the tissue. Andrew looked surprised and observed, not asking a question. She dipped the fork multiple times making noise from the chinaware. She wrote "My pasta - you! your chicken - me?". By the time she finished painting the words on the tissue delicately, she realized her idea of a proposal was the stupidest thing she had ever done in her life and immediately crushed it into her fist.

'What's wrong?' Andrew asked, throwing his hands in the air.

'Nothing.' She threw the tissue to the left corner of the table which Andrew couldn't reach.

'Listen, be sure to take your tablets regularly.' Andrew gave all his suggestions after losing his patience by waiting for her to finish whatever she was concentratedly doing. They both spoke about various things while they ate, Andrew felt a natural comfort in their conversation, unlike before. After lunch, Samantha left the table first, but Andrew did not forget the tissue. He reached it easily by stretching his right leg forward. He delicately cleared the wrinkles to reveal the text. He was confused at first, then realized what she would've meant. Andrew felt his feet lighten, almost like flying.

CHAPTER 24

Samantha appeared as a freshly bloomed flower wrapped in her pale pink shirt. Her semi-curled hair fell effortlessly surrounding her radiant cheeks. The sun made her slight dark circles prominent which she had grown from the improper sleep patterns, which Andrew felt were attractive. Right outside the restaurant, Andrew saw Samantha shuffling here and there, trying to escape from a stray dog who flaunted his cuteness to earn some food for himself. Andrew slowly drove the car from the parking lot, not taking his eyes off that irresistible sight. Samantha returned to the car with tiny jumps.

Andrew took a moment to grasp the whole scene in his eyes. 'You look beautiful.' He couldn't resist telling her. Goosebumps raised across Samantha's arm as soon as she heard it. She twisted and turned behind the seat belt hearing his compliment. This was the first time ever she had received such a compliment, according to her memory. She felt too shy to respond. They were surrounded by love and were shrunk with shyness.

Samantha came up with a random question desperately wanting to get relieved from the tension. 'So, where do you live in Bangalore? Is it close to my house?'

'Not really. My house is in Richmond Town, but my clinic is pretty close to your house. And we also share the same church. Remember? That is where I saw you the first time.' She nodded. 'You were in a white Kurti, a loose ponytail, your nose and lips almost the same colour, and your eyes, they have a charm hidden in there.'

Samantha was impressed with the level of detail. She slowly looked into Andrew's eyes, the thought of not seeing him anymore wrenched her heart. 'And?'

'And what?'

'No dormitory, no Sam, no dealing with my nuisance anymore. You'll be quite relieved, won't you?'

'I really have no thoughts of what my future days are going to be like. But I'm sure I cannot be without visiting you.'

She sighed. 'I will miss you.' Her voice broke while she gripped her moist palm over his forearm.

He held her hand softly, 'Hey, it's going to be fine.'

Tears rolled from her eyes. 'I was so stupid to call my dad. I didn't know what I was doing. And what am I going to do without you? I'm really scared, Andrew.'

He pulled over the car on the side of the lane. He took both of her hands into his. 'Look at me. Hey, look at me. You'll be alright. You'll do great, actually. Look forward to your future, you need to do a lot of things. I promise I will check on you every day. Now, relax.' He wiped the tears on her cheeks away. He pulled her closer by holding her arm and hugged her sideways. 'You're a warrior, Sam. You've faced big things. You can handle this.' He held her face in his palms. Their eyes met briefly for a minute. 'Listen. I...'

Andrew refrained from the urge to say the three golden words. I believe in you. That was what he said instead and smoothly kissed her forehead. She felt nervous, and better at the same time. Samantha and Andrew felt the joy of their untold love around them. They wished that moment would last eternally, without having to deal with the chaos of life anymore. They both fell back to their seats, Samantha leaned against the window that reflected herself, slipped into dreaming a future with Andrew, enjoying the mild beats ringing behind her head.

They stayed stagnant in their seats for several minutes, staring at the entrance after reaching Samantha's house. Andrew eventually got out of the car and held the door for Samantha. She gradually stepped down from the car, wiping the tears that emerged uncontrollably onto her cheeks. The look she gave Andrew, straight into his eyes, intensified their feelings. She clasped him tightly in her arms. Andrew could not be just a doctor or a well-wisher at that moment. He reciprocated the hug just like he wanted to all this while ago. Andrew and Samantha let themselves be honest, without any filters for their emotions. At that moment, Andrew felt the most content in his life. He held her face in the middle of his palms and slowly pressed his lips against hers. He started to kiss the side of her cheeks, gradually pecked across her face, and kissed her lips again, this time tighter. Samantha's heartbeat elevated, and she felt heat waves across arms and feet. They both conveyed their love without having to say a word.

'Go. I'll surely come for you,' he whispered in her ear.

She's really leaving, Andrew told himself. He watched her walk under the warm lights toward her home. The growing distance between them felt like miles. His palms sweated; he felt his heart pumping to explode with each and every step she took.

'Sam!' he screamed, running towards her. 'First compartment.' He pointed at the suitcase she held, 'First compartment has all your medicines. You know, right? Take them without fail. Eat well. Okay?' he panted.

'Okay. Aren't you coming?' She turned and looked at the entrance.

'No... I'll need to visit the clinic. You can text or call me anytime. Okay?'

She nodded. 'Take care. Bye, Andy.'

CHAPTER 25

Samantha did not anticipate the timidity she would develop when she called her father the day before. She'd been at the peak of an emotional toll since Andrew had said that they were nearing home during the drive. She stood by the metal gate, capturing the whole picture of her home. She felt the weight of mountains tied to her feet while she stepped forward. Andrew wanted her to take her own time, as this was indeed a big step considering the whole chaos she had gone through. With her own family waiting eagerly behind the unopened door, she looked back at Andrew who stood by his car, hands crossed.

She gradually approached the entrance, crossed the gate as if entering an unknown place for the first time, climbed the three steps, and rang the calling bell with trembling fingers. She couldn't not notice the empty space that used to be a place for Simon's bike. Victor opened the door within a few seconds before she could fall into the pit of thoughts, he'd been waiting on his toes behind the door for her arrival. He gave a deep sigh of relief looking at his daughter. He ran his hand across her face with his eyes still and dilated.

'Oh! Sam, you're here. My baby is here,' cried Layla. She grabbed Samantha in a tight embrace, almost crushing her bones. Samantha stayed still as her parents expressed their happiness of seeing her after three long months. *They have gotten old, older than what I remember.* She turned back to see if Andrew was still there but only saw the empty road.

'Sam, wait, I'll bring some water. Or, would you like to have something hot?' Layla hurried up.

'Let her freshen up, we all shall eat dinner together,' Victor interrupted hopefully.

Samantha felt everything new. Her home, her parents, her room, her wardrobe, she felt everything foreign and did not dare to touch. At the table, Samantha's plate was filled with various dishes, two varieties of meat gravies, stir-fried vegetables, one salad, roti, and papad. She barely touched any of it. 'Eat up, darling, you should be hungry,' her mother caressed.

'I... I'm not really hungry.' Samantha avoided making eye contact.

'Not hungry?' Layla was pretty upset with Samantha's denial of the food which she herself cooked.

'How are you dear?' Victor asked. She nodded in response. She only gave brief movements.

'How is Andrew?'

'He's fine.'

'Look, we're sorry. I know you must be upset that we haven't visited you all this while.' Samantha frowned. Victor continued, 'But there's a lot for you to know. You'll be in a position to understand then.'

Samantha stayed quiet; her sight fixed on the glass jar filled with water in front of her. Her mind was completely occupied by Andrew. His tender kiss did not leave her thoughts. She remembered the butterflies that wandered when he touched her.

'Are you okay?' Victor shouted.

'Han.' Samantha nodded in shock. She felt surreal to find herself home. She felt deprived of the solitude she'd had at the dormitory, predominantly the presence of Andrew. In a split second, she also recalled how much she had missed her family while she was away. She smiled at the contentment her parents' faces bore.

Samantha did not, rather could not answer any of her parents' questions. After dinner, she locked herself in her room. She took time to slowly walk around and observe, the art piece of the letter "S" she had threaded on a board of needles, the reading desk with books neatly piled upon, and her wardrobe, and finally the large square area on the wall next to the desk, stuck with numerous pictures of herself along with Simon. She was dumbstruck looking at the wall of pictures. She hunched to take a detailed look at each picture without touching them. The pictures ranged right from their childhood. She smiled looking at a few familiar pictures; like the one with Simon lifting her up on his shoulder, the both of them riding bicycles on a summer evening; Victor holding both of them close where Samantha reached his hip and Simon to his shoulder. Samantha's eyes were stuck on one picture that she felt was taken from her recent memory.

She carefully picked the picture off the wall. She ran her fingers across Simon's face, clearing the thin layer of dust cast upon the soft film layer. Her heart shrunk as Simon's face got visibly clearer. It was a picture taken when he had started his first job when Samantha was sixteen years old. Simon folded his left arm across her neck from behind and was pretending to hit her head with his right hand. 'Wait for a couple of years and I will reach beyond you.' She smiled and recalled what she had said when the picture was clicked. *This feels like yesterday*, she thought. *If this feels like yesterday... how would my yesterday have looked like? What would I have forgotten? I really wanna know.*

Samantha stood in front of the picture wall lost in thoughts about her lost memory. Her phone hissed when she was about to sink into her own sorrow. **All settled?** It was Andrew. Her eyes went wider looking at the notification.

She took the picture to bed along with her. She leaned her back on the pillow resting on the headboard with the phone in her right hand and the picture in her left.

'Andrew!!! I miss you,' she initially typed. Backspaced it and typed **Andrew!!! I'm okay. What about you?** Her fingers shuffled on the keypad with her eyes wide.

My place is quite filthy. Just dusted my bedroom. Gotta clean the whole house early tomorrow.

It seems I've forgotten a lot of things. I feel strange and sad. I don't remember how I used to converse with my mom and dad. And… they look so different from what I remember. I don't remember a bit of them growing old. Andrew! I'm afraid my life will remain this way going forward. :-(

Tears rolled while she put her feelings into words. The fact that Andrew was not around made her emotionally vulnerable. She received a call from him within a moment after she sent the message.

Hi, can I talk to Samantha?

Samantha's well-controlled tears burst out as soon as she heard the soothing voice of her love. 'I'm scared. I don't want to live my life like this. Not remembering anything that happened. I want my memory back.' She wept.

It's not even a day since you got home. You're with your parents now. Everything falls into place, and the same applies to your memory. It will happen. In our hands lies an opportunity to give a positive approach. So now, I want you to think positively and look at the brighter side. Memory will come when it has to come,

I promise it will come sooner than you think. Would you do two things which I'm gonna tell you to get your memory back?

What?

Go take your tablets and get some good sleep.

Will I get my memory back if I take those tablets?

Of course, my dear. Tomorrow is a new day, it's a new start. I'll visit you for sure as I promised. Now go to bed. Please.

Ok, Samantha said reluctantly.

Great. I know you're a strong girl.

Hmmn.

Tuck yourself. Get some sleep. Good night!

Good night. That night Samantha quarrelled with her thoughts as long as she could and slept holding the phone and the photo close to her hoping for a new day.

When Samantha woke up, she was startled to see her dad sitting on the wooden chair paired with her studying table. Victor had a long-lost look in his eyes. Samantha quickly rubbed her eyes for a clear vision and witnessed her dad looking at her with a grin.

'Good morning, dear!'

She jumped into a sitting position not being used to a base and intimidating voice in the morning. She spied on the wall clock opposite her just for a second to learn that it was fifteen minutes past eleven. 'Good morning!' she forced a half smile.

'What would you like to have? Coffee as always?'

'No! Just water. I'll drink coffee after meditation'

'Well, great! Layla, please bring some water,' Victor cried right from where he was sitting, startling Samantha again.

'Warm! Warm water.'

'yeah, WARM WATER!' he again cried.

'Okay!' Layla reciprocated.

'Did you sleep well?' Victor tried to tune his voice as politely as possible. She nodded in response. 'Good'

'Good morning, darling! Here, warm water.' Layla was like a lightning bolt entering and leaving the room.

'Okay, You freshen up. Let's have breakfast together. After that, we'll be going to the church, so dress accordingly,' Victor said while leaving the room sparing some time for herself.

The sunrays thrust into the room from the middle of the sheets that covered the entrance to the balcony. Samantha was awed by the balcony space she totally forgot and did not notice the previous night. She visited the balcony sipping the warm water from the ceramic cup.

She allowed the sun to seep into her skin, though the heat pricked her a bit. She also missed the sea view from the dormitory. Right when she remembered the sea, Andrew struck her mind. She took her phone and slid her finger from the top-notch to find a message notification from Andrew. "I'm sure I did not miss you last night."

She frowned upon reading the clueless text from Andrew sent as early as 8 a.m. "Really?"

A response came within a minute. "Yeah! Because you were all my dreams…"

A cheer travelled from her heart to her eyes leaving a smile in between. "Wow!"

"I hope everything's fine!"

"I think so. Dad wants to take me to the church."

"Amazing! Call me whenever you need. I have some formalities to be done at the hospital. I'll finish that and come to visit you." Samantha felt a thunder of energy travel throughout her body just at the thought of Andrew visiting her.

After freshening up, Samantha took a few minutes to go through her wardrobe collection. Apparently, she did not remember any of her clothes. She searched specifically for ethnic wear within the western wardrobe. After turning the whole wardrobe inside-out, she found a red Kurti which passed her expectations.

The dining table was decorated with colourful dishes filled with a variety of food. She could make up a few of them with minimal judgment; there were rice cakes, rice pancakes, and string hoppers, and she could guess only one gravy which was vegetable stew. She recalled that string hoppers with vegetable stew was one of the favorite breakfasts since her childhood.

'Come, come!' Layla invited as she placed a chinaware plate in front of Samantha. The mother and daughter shared a look of contentment and a short smile. 'What would you like to have? I made Malabar-style chicken gravy, this would taste brilliantly with the rice cakes, shall I serve?' Layla's eyes went wide. 'Here, have this with rice pancakes, this will be amazing.' Layla almost served the curry.

'No.' Samantha obstructed her mother's hand holding the ladle. 'I'm not used to eating that. I will eat string hoppers and vegetable stew.'

An awkward silence passed when Samantha denied the food which was her usual favorite before her memory was gone. She declared that the food options at the dormitory were always vegetarian and that she will be more comfortable savouring them. 'Let her eat whatever she wants.' Victor normalized.

CHAPTER 26

The commute to the church made Samantha nostalgic about her drive with Andrew from Chennai. Victor showed Samantha her favorite ice cream place which offers disc ice creams with all the flavours of natural fruits.

'Ice cream?' Both peered at the ice cream parlour with a grin. Samantha was surprised to have recollected her childhood memories in that ice cream shop. she remembered that after finishing every maths exam in school, she would get ice cream as a reward.

'Banana?' Her eyes widened. She swallowed as her memories gave away the taste from just the thought of it. Victor jumped out of the car dynamically to give his little daughter an ice cream treat after a long time. *I hope Andrew comes soon*, she thought. *I have to show him my favorite ice cream parlour. Oh, how nice to have one together. Damn. I don't even know what his favorite ice cream flavour is. I'm sure there is much more I need to learn about him.* She smirked. While she spoke to herself, she saw a person whose face looked familiar. There used to be a young boy selling boiled peanuts in a small stall. Now, the stall was upgraded to a shop, and the young boy had developed into a man with a neatly groomed beard. She felt genuinely happy about his progressive life.

Memories flipped in her head. She was excited to see someone familiar from her memory, other than her parents. She out of the car immediately to meet him and ask if he also remembered her. The shop was on the opposite side of the two-way road. She stood at the edge of the tarred road, amidst fastly passing vehicles, struggling to cross to the other end. She felt friction on her hand pulling backward, and her whole body swirled back twice, flipping her hair, landing against the car, her head did not stop revolving even after her body.

'Dood, where've you been all this while? Boss and I were searching for you all over Bangalore, man. We really missed you!' cried a tall person, as if they were old friends.

Samantha took a moment to stand steady. She noticed the tall person with a frown. She despised his clumsy beard and the ponytail tied at the back of his head for only a little hair. Before she could answer the unexpected stranger, she heard her name screamed out by her father from the other side of the lane. Victor ran, escaping the vehicles without waiting for the signal.

'Hi, uncle!' the stranger wished casually. While Victor finally reached with an ice cream in his hand.

'Hey! What have I told you?' Victor clenched the stranger's arm and dragged him far away, until Samantha couldn't hear their conversation. They spoke continuously without breathing space; it definitely did not go the polite way. Samantha stared at them like a stalker. Her head hurt. She slowly realized that she hit the car when the stranger pulled her back.

She saw her dad struggle to control the tall person with one hand holding her ice cream. The stranger spoke pointing at the car. She stared at him, trying to remember if she knew the person. He looked too young to consider a friend of her father and too weird looking to consider a friend of hers. Sweat oozed out of Samantha's forehead. She squeezed her fist several times. The pointing and yelling of the stranger seemed like he wanted to catch hold of Samantha for something she did in the past, but her father fought against him not allowing him to get even an inch closer to her. Samantha's heart rate stayed high constantly looking at the scene, for she realized that she was still not ready to tackle situations like these. She was agitated and scared by the time Victor returned to the car.

'What, what happened?' Samantha babbled.

'Nothing, seems he lost something. Just don't bother.'

'No! I think he knows me. I might've forgotten. Did you ask him for details?'

'Look, there will be many instances like these, you should learn to ignore them.' He sounded tensed.

Samantha refrained from asking more questions. The scenes revolved around her head in tiny imaginary objects, worsening the ache. Her headache persisted even after entering the church. She walked through the aisle holding her father's hand like a little girl. Her expanded pupils took in all the details of the painted glasses, which illustrated important life events of Jesus. The priest prayed with his eyes closed and so chorused the crowd. She felt a constant twinge on her head where she got hurt. The tall stranger's face haunted her every time she closed her eyes to blink. Scenes of him talking flashed in her mind, but she couldn't figure out if those are just her mind imagining things.

Numerous questions popped into her head. *Who is he? I'm sure he knows me. That is how he spoke. Like he knew me for a very long time. I'm sure Dad also knows. But why did he stop him from talking to me? He said someone else was also searching for me. His name was... he said... Gosh, I couldn't even remember exactly what happened ten minutes ago, how can I recall a person who totally seems a stranger to me?* Samantha gazed into the eyes of mother Mary for a prolonged period. *Do you even exist? Does any of these prayers make sense to you?*

She was taken back to an incident from the past when she'd asked exactly the same questions. It was when she miserably performed her maths board exam and had prayed for some miracle to happen. The next day a news flashed up all over the media that the maths board exam answer sheets were accidentally burnt and all the students were graded upon their practice tests.

Samantha believed that that instance was the answer for her prayers. She did not take her eyes off mother Mary and said, '*Mother, I know you can make miracles happen. All I'm asking for is my past. I cannot live like this anymore. I feel like I'm lost in a forest with hundreds of paths branching around me. I don't know what is true or what is my imagination. I am not able to deal with the dilemma anymore. Would you tell me what happened? Please! Please give me my past.*'

'Hello, Victor. I see Samantha is back. Is she alright now?' asked Peter, one of Victor's friends, approaching them from the dispersed crowd. *He has gotten too old and fat,* she thought, *What do you mean am I alright now? When was I not? Firstly, what's wrong with you and your belly, Uncle Peter?*

'Hi, yeah she's absolutely fine.'

'I believe no more mood swings, no more tantrums. Am I right, Samantha? Be kind to your parents, alright?' Peter said with a smirk, dropping his chin close to his chest and looking at her over his glasses. Samantha frowned upon treating her like an abnormal turned into a normal.

'No, no, nothing as such. We actually got some work to be done. See you, Peter.' Victor hurried explicitly, grabbing Samantha's hand. The visit to the church gave Samantha agony rather than peace. After a long refrain, she spoke up while going back home, 'What was wrong with Daddy?'

Victor could not help but quietly cherish his daughter addressing him as 'daddy' for the first time after returning home. He did not answer the question though.

'Daddy, Andrew did tell me that I went through depression, and these people don't know about that, do they? I don't think he was referring to that though. Why should he ask me to be kind? What have I done?'

'If you're worried about Peter's words, then please ignore them. You need not answer anybody.' Victor's response did not seem to answer her question.

'Answering others was not my concern. I was expecting only two words from you Daddy, that nothing was wrong! If that's not your answer, I can't understand what it is.'

He swallowed, not able to take his words back. She stayed quiet all along the journey and locked herself up in her room after getting home.

Later that day, the moment Samantha was most expecting happened; Andrew visited. Following the things that happened that morning, Samantha did not want to see anybody, including Andrew.

'Sam!' her mother screamed from the other side of the door. 'Samantha, Andrew came to visit you. Please open the door.' Samantha's blood rushed to her face upon hearing that name

'Sam? Hope everything's okay.' Victor tapped the door twice.. She quickly approached the door but did not open it.

'It's okay if you want to stay inside. We can talk like this.' Andrew leaned against the door. Goosebumps erupted all over her bare arms as his voice got closer. She came closer to the door. The urge to look at his face wrenched her heart.

'Sam.' Butterflies fluttered in her belly. 'How are you?' he asked with the warmest voice ever that melted her heart. She opened the door slowly to see him sitting near the door, alone. She felt a sense of calm with his presence. She walked to the balcony, and so he followed. Her heart grew heavier in the comfort of his caress against her head with mild strokes. Her eyes overflowed.

'Oh, no. No. Don't.' He pushed away the hair falling from her eyes. 'You're fine, Sam. It's okay.'

'No. it's not. It's not okay. We should've stayed back in Chennai.'

'What happened? What are you so upset about?'

'It's me. I wasn't alright. Peter Uncle… uncle said that I was hurting people. I'm sure I did something to hurt my parents. And someone came to me to talk, an old friend maybe. I strongly feel that I've seen him somewhere. But I don't remember. I'm just here, ready to start a new life with all the mess I created in the past. There are loads of questions in my mind to which I have no answer. Do you know how it feels? It feels hopeless. Yes, that is how I feel now. My parents had some idea of what I like and what I don't, of course; they've seen me since I was born, but that is not how I am right now. She made chicken curry in the morning and said it's my favorite. What should I tell her? Chicken? Yuck, I don't want to eat a dead animal. Well, that is what came to my mind. These might be small things for you, Andrew. I cannot deal with these differences and uncertainty.' She collapsed, hugging her knees at the very place she was standing.

'Well, you could've just asked them to save it for me!' Andrew said with a husky voice. Samantha and Andrew shared a moment of eye contact and burst into laughter. Samantha leaped and hugged him as tight as possible. Andrew let her agony fume away in the warmth of their hug.

The moment broke with the tapping on the door. 'Lunch is ready.' Layla informed from the other side.

Samantha raised her head with wet eyes. Andrew's heart melted looking at his love with so much pain in her eyes. When she tried to retract herself from Andrew's warmth, he clenched her wrist and pulled her closer. He locked his lips against hers and they both dwelled in a cloud of love. Andrew could not think of a better way to assure his love and support her feelings. He knew that nothing could ever stop him from showing love to her as they were no longer doctor and patient. His gesture meant everything to her at that moment, she felt rest assured that everything was going to be okay and that he would be there for her no matter what. After the extended exchange of love, their heads tipped against each other gently with wide grins on their faces.

That night, Samantha protested while Andrew left her place. She stared with wet eyes until his car left her sight far away. She replayed the kiss they shared in her head numerous times; his lips were as smooth as butter, his breath fresh, the gentle gesture of his tongue. *How perfect. Is this called the perfect kiss? If there were a contest for a perfect kisser, I would definitely recommend Andrew.* She giggled at her own joke.

Whilst Samantha dwelled in Andrew's memories, a thought came over her all at once. She was dragged by an inner force straight to the writing table and opened the drawer like it was something instructed to her in her head. She found a few books stuffed, and a set of pens and pencils lying next to them. She stared at the table for a few moments to remember why she'd opened the drawer. She closed it and got back in bed. Memories tried to reach her. She blinked at the writing table sitting at the edge of her bed, trying to fathom what just happened. She again opened the drawer and emptied the contents. She tried to remove the seamless white cardboard base that fit at the bottom and was shocked to reveal an extra chamber underneath. She gasped, and pins and needles ran through her spine.

CHAPTER 27

Memories are our footsteps. We live them. We create them. We go past them; for at some point in life, we need to pause and look back at our footsteps to know where we have come from. Good or bad, these were created by us and cannot be erased.

Two big cigarette boxes, one white and the other brown; several small plastic zip-lock packets containing dried, brownish, tiny broccoli-like chunks. The packets were covered with clustered cobwebs and dust. Samantha jumped onto her bed at the sight. Her eyes did not shift from the opened drawer. She remembered seeing these dried leaves in movies, but could not remember what they were. She approached the table again to take a detailed look. She took the cigarette pack with trembling hands and inspected it to identify the opening. She held the box in one hand, poked her nail in the visible small gap near the flap, and pulled it open. She was surprised to see the box half empty. *Who would've kept this here? How did I even know that there was a chamber underneath? But, mom said this is my room. Was Simon using my room secretly?*

Her eyes widened at the probability, as she knew for sure that the only person who smoked in that house was her brother. She kept the cigarette pack in the same place and covered the drawer with books as before. She knocked on her parent's bedroom door.

'Come in, Sam!' her mother voiced from inside.

'Did somebody else use my room when I wasn't here?'

'NO!' answered Mr. and Mrs. Victor simultaneously.

'Okay...' She hesitated to inquire about Simon.

'What happened? Anything wrong?' Victor frowned, rising from his sleeping position.

'No, nothing. Did Bunny share my bedroom in the past?' Her face warmed up.

Layla chuckled before answering, 'It has always been you hanging out in his room. All the time. You would go to your room only to sleep.' Her mother's answer blew an explosion in her heart. She stood still at the very place lost in thoughts. 'Do you want me to sleep with you?' Layla asked, holding Samantha by her shoulder which brought her back from the void.

'No. no. I'm fine.' She faked a shrug and got back to her room swiftly.

It was only me. I lived in this room. Then who would've hidden them here? Did we buy this table second-hand?

Who am I kidding, I have been seeing this table since I was a kid. She chewed on her nails. She damned herself for not having a clue about the foreign objects in her room. She tutted, holding her right temple, due to the headache that she was enduring since that morning. She sat on the bed leaning on one side resting her head on the wall. Her eyes closed gradually. She had fallen asleep for almost an hour before she was struck by a comet in her head. Her red eyes opened in what felt like a blink; they weren't stable.

Her head still hurt with a constant throb banging at the centre. The humming noise of the fan almost ripped her in two. She dropped her head in her arms due to unbearable torment. She felt the moment surreal as scenes from her past lined up in front of her eyes, running like a movie. She stood on the floor with gripped feet, holding her head tight as she remembered the past. She re-lived old places, old scents, and old habits over again. She clenched her hair with both the palms with all her strength while the memories unfolded rapidly. She trembled in shock and stayed curled up in the same place for several hours until she was able to open her eyes. She held her racing chest in an attempt to regulate her breathing. Her eyes oozed unstoppable tears.

'NO. NO.' She slapped herself with both her palms. She slowly crawled to the picture wall. She steadied herself to stand by taking support of the wall; however, stood only with her legs bent. She took the pictures in to her hand one by one. His voice echoed in her ears calling her name; she could hear his laughter, could smell cigarettes and charts which filled his space, could sense his touch. Her heart bled for the one who loved her unconditionally, the one who guided her like a guru, cared for her like a father, the one who lost his life at stake over a silly bet she had hooked him to. 'I'm sorry.'

She knelt in front of the numerous pictures, 'I'm sorry, Bunny. It's all my fault. My fault.' Guilt swallowed her. She despised herself for still being alive. Her eyes went wider when the thought of taking her life away possessed her completely.

CHAPTER 28

The room swirled before her eyes. She darted across the corners of the room with no control, holding whichever she could find for balance. She blinked, closing her eyelids tight, and buried her head in between her palms as if to protect it from blowing away.

She felt suffocated and ran to the balcony. She gasped, taking large breaths through her mouth. She collapsed at one corner of the balcony. She closed her eyes tight while a smile dwelled in her memories, a well-known fuller smile with prominent front teeth.

'Bunny...' The smile disappeared within a moment; Bunny looked as a completely grown man which she always strived to remember. She was mesmerized to look at his vivid eyes. 'I bet I'll hit the tip of your head in a minute. Losers should make coffee.' She saw him scream and run towards her. She ran with a pink blood-rushed face, her eyes all wide and thrilled while Simon chased her behind.

She nodded fiercely with her eyes closed and said 'This! This is us.' A tear rolled over her cheek while she shivered in the cold breeze. She flinched as she felt the intensity of him slapping, and within a heartbeat an infinite amount of memories piled up in her head adding a pound each. Hundreds of landmines bust in her head as the past unfolded. She felt bizarre about her memories but knew that they were true. Her eyes stalled, holding her breath as she learned how Simon died.

'I…I-I did.' She clenched her neck and slapped herself on both her cheeks several times.

'GO!'

She heard a voice. She looked around and found herself at one corner of the balcony. Outside, she witnessed only a few sparkling dots laid across the pitch-black sky. She tried focusing on the hazy image of the old water tank which wasn't clearly seen from her balcony. 'GO. GO,' her inner self insisted. She picked up her hoodie, layered it upon her pajamas, and stepped out of her house. This time she knew where she was heading. She walked, batting away the thick mist, awestricken by the similarly curled-up dogs sleeping across the streets. She flinched at the rats crossing by.

The old water tank was banned years ago following the multiple suicides that happened by the school and college students. Every time the news flashed out to the colony, Samantha would stare at the tank from her balcony and wonder how these people got the courage to even climb that height and why would someone take their life away for whatever reason it might hold. She thought it was an insane thing that people could ever do with their lives. Now she was heading to the same spot to do the same insane thing she criticized.

Her eyes followed the stairs that led to the tank through the huge concrete pillars; her head bent parallel to the ground almost crushing the back of her neck. She held the cold cement railing that gave shivers all over her body. She took a couple of minutes, sighed deeply, and took the first step. She gradually climbed the stairs with trembling footsteps. It got colder as she climbed. The cold misty breeze hit right on her face. She halted, her heart raced at once when she heard Simon's voice calling her name. She looked around the land at the low altitude. She swallowed a couple of times scared to move forward. She again heard the voice calling her name. 'Bunny?' she mumbled. The moment she uttered his name, she knew how much she missed her brother. Her heart wrenched, and tears flowed uncontrollably. She sat in the middle of the stairs and sobbed for several minutes.

'Bunny… Bunny,' she chanted. She knew that she was stuck in the middle of the stairs of a huge unmaintained concrete water tank and wanted to move forward. She slowly closed her eyes and recalled Andrew's instructions to breathe in and breathe out, controlling her breathing. Simon's face refused to leave her eyes. She realized she never visited the place where Simon was buried. Her eyes popped out. She thought she needed to visit Simon at that very moment no matter what. She descended the stairs slowly, holding the cold railing tight with the fear of slipping.

She followed the route it took to reach the graveyard, as if led by her muscle memory. Not a single time before had she felt the heavy heart of going to a cemetery. She recalled going there every year, unemotionally and casually on her grandfather's death anniversary. She walked for more than the expected time wondering if she was going on the right path. She was relieved looking at the familiar name board with a brief text on it surrounded by maintained bushes. The place was poorly lighted with only one tall lamp post at the wide, rusted entrance gate. She peered and was disappointed to see the gates locked. She clenched upon the cold, filthy gates and gazed across various tombstones. 'Where are you? Where are you, Bunny? See, I've come to see you. I want to see you right now. Appear in front of me right now. I would like to come along with you, Bunny. Please.'

She peered inside through the narrow gaps of the rusted gates to see if there was any other entrance. The fog blocked part of her view. She hugged herself by tucking her hands in the front pockets of the hoodie. A slight ray of light appeared in the sky giving the signs of dawn. She stared at the three lanes that branched into the cemetery, waiting for someone who could open the gates.

Layla couldn't sleep after the early hours that day and got up earlier than usual to fix breakfast for the family. She slowly walked to the entrance, tying her hair up, to check if the milk had arrived yet. She became motionless for a few moments, horrified, looking at the door open already. 'Victor!' She ran back into the bedroom. 'Victor, wake up. Victor!' She jolted him with her utmost strength.

'Wha... What happened?'

'The door is open. Did you lock it last night?' she panted, with eyes wide open.

'What?' He raised his head. 'Did you check on Sam?'

She gasped.

'Come.' They both rushed to find Samantha's room empty. Layla visited all the tables and books, looking for any notes, while Victor ran in and around the building including the vicinity only to realize that they had lost their daughter once again.

CHAPTER 29

Samantha saw a ray of light approaching her. Slowly, an old man with a completely gray beard and marbled hair appeared. He was wearing a dull, brown T-shirt paired with black track pants. He gave brief eye contact with Samantha, his forehead wrinkled, which intimidated her. Her palms sweated, she also wanted to make sure that he was an actual human, but she couldn't get a voice out of her throat.

'Miss, do you need any help?' he asked with a slightly shaky voice. *Yes, he is human.*

'Can you… can you open these? She moved closer to the middle of the gate.

'Are you a visitor?'

'Yes!' she nodded.

'You… are you alone? How long were you waiting?' His voice became clearer as he approached 'It is too early to get in.'

She stayed still while his words travelled slowly to her head and to her consciousness. 'NO,' she exasperatedly sighed. She reached for the gate again and blinked to look beyond the little source of light.

Out of his experience in life, he could perceive Samantha's pain from that one act.

'For now, come with me.' His eyes sparked. The old man walked beyond the visible fence, leading to a broken area in the middle of the cemetery.

'Would you like to make use of this?' He pointed at the narrow opening covered with mud. She looked intently at the path. 'I come here every morning; this is the path I use. C'mon, I'll help you.' He stretched his left hand to hold her. She held his hand and jumped sideways across the path. As soon as she entered, she darted across the series of graves and tombstones, stopping when she realized she didn't know where Simon's grave was placed. She took a moment, sighed, and glanced at the vast count of tombs laid surrounding her. She rushed back to the old man. 'Do you know where Simon's grave is?'

'Whose?' He bent forward, placing his hand back on one of his ears.

'Simon Sebastian.'

'Nope. Sorry. Is it recent, I mean...'

She shook her head. Standing at the centre of the countless tombs, she wondered which one represented the remains of her brother. Just when she was about to break down hopelessly, she noticed the old man bending down with squinted eyes, checking out for the last name on the tombs with the help of his torchlight. She rushed shuffling between the tombs, not missing checking back on the old man constantly. She breathed hard, inhaling the earthy cold air and exhaling a tiny cloud that instantly disappeared.

'Miss.' The old man waved at Samantha. Her heart dropped for a moment hearing the deep voice from far across the other end of the cemetery. She slowly approached him, with her palms and temples sweating like never before despite the cold environment. The glimpse of a tall, white-painted grave that appeared from the light of his torch had dug memories from her childhood. That belonged to Rodger Sebastian, Samantha's grandfather. She could recall her and her brother playing in and around this grave while their parents prayed.

'I think I found it,' said the old man, moving a step aside, revealing a pitch-black grave made of granite. She read the glowing silver letters engraved on the tombstone not moving closer.

Simon Sebastian

1988 - 2018

A MAN OF INTELLIGENCE

A SON OF BENEVOLENCE

A BROTHER OF LENIENCE

Her knees weakened, she collapsed on the ground; her hands shivered and her jaw dropped. She sucked in a breath of sob. The old man was dumbfound to look at Samantha in such situation, he waited until she settled. Draining her sorrow partially, she crawled up to the black representation of her brother. Her eyes were barely open when she touched the silver name with her trembling hands. 'I…' she choked up on her words. 'I beg you to come back.' She poked her fingers at his name. Her eyes were filled with guilt, lips shivered as she spoke. 'I'm sorry…' Tears burst across her cheeks.

The old man was heart rendered looking at Samantha. 'I know that I cannot lessen your pain in any way,' he said, 'but I'm pretty sure that his soul is at peace.' He caressed her head. His intervention reminded her that she was not alone. She gently sat straight on her knees, rubbing her face with the back of her forearms.

'How is uh…' He focused the torch on the silver letters and said, 'Simon related to you?'

'My– my brother.' Her voice was mournful.

'Oh. I'm sorry for the loss.'

She stared at Simon's name quietly.

'I suppose you're visiting for the first time?' she nodded.

'Hmm.' He sat down facing her. 'Over there,' he continued talking, pointing somewhere near the gate, 'is my son's grave. I lost him at a significant time, when he was thirty-two, right when I wanted to hand over my business to him and more importantly, when he was just about to get married. It couldn't have gone worse than that.' He stayed quiet for several moments, lost in his thoughts.

'How?' Her voice startled the old man.

'In a vacation. It was bad weather and yet, he along with his friends attempted paragliding. Everyone was safe, except him. Something malfunctioned, they said, my son and the instructor both died on the spot.' *At least you're not the reason,* her inner self crucified her. 'It has been quite some time. I thought I could cope with it and moved to Bombay to continue to look after my business. But… you know, well, I'm sure you should be knowing by now with your parents having lost one of their children. Kids can recover and build a life after a parent's loss, but a parent can never sort out their life.' He wiped a tear that just slipped onto his cheeks. Her eyes widened, almost skipping a beat. His words shook her deep inside. The pain of proving her conscience wrong punched her in the gut. Her world was literally flipped upside down, from wrong to right.

'A parent puts their time and blood into making his child's life easier,' he continued talking, 'and if the child is no more, it's all pointless. I left the business soon after and moved here. Where my son is. I come here every morning, touch his grave, revisit some memories, and just wait for my time to meet him.' His eyes twinkled again. Samantha's eyes were fixed on the old man for an extended period, her mind in an elaborated rationalizing process. She rose up and stepped back, gradually placing her right foot first with a stern look. The old man also steadied himself and stepped up to his heels. Samantha, meanwhile, was almost five feet away.

'Are you okay?' He frowned.

'I've to go… thank you so much, sir.'

She ran beyond the broken metal fence, with all the strength she had at that moment, with the breeze hitting on her face, talking to herself about the things she hadn't thought about before.

Who was he? Did I actually have a conversation with him? Well, I don't know, I've never seen him before and I don't think I will ever see him again. But he has no idea about what he did to me now. Why? Why in the world did I not think about all this till now? I, Samantha, sister of a late brother who has spent most of his life amusing me and teaching me, daughter of the parents who still treat me normal in spite of giving them the horrible pain by depriving them from their perfect son, attempted suicide, got addicted to drugs, and even tried to run away from home. Lover of a person who would change his entire world for me. Friend of a person who could stand against the world for me. A woman who has seen most of the virtue of men has a purpose to live. From now on, every fleeting minute in my life will be spent to pay them back.

Samantha sprinted from the cemetery across the quiet lanes in the dawned light. The fresh, cold breeze hit her face, radiating clarity in her thoughts. Her lips drew wider to have realized that she could make her parents' life happier. A tide of hope aroused in her. Her legs crossed each other within nanoseconds as she ran with all her energy. She screamed her guts out closing her eyes tighter in the joy of having had her feelings and decisions in line after what felt like a lifetime.

All of a sudden, it felt like a thunderstorm hit from head to toe. She was knocked down to the ground, falling three feet away and rolling in the mud within a blink after hitting the metal pole. Her heart palpitated, and she swayed left to right in pain holding her right temple as hard as possible. She struggled to open her eyes and could look only with a narrow vision through her lashes. She pictured hugging her parents tight, kissing Andrew and creating a family with all of them together. Her desire made her crawl up slowly in the mud to at least reach the corner of the street. She passed out in the middle of the unpopular street that led to the cemetery, feeling her soul leaving the body.

CHAPTER 30

Andrew tutted, squinting his eyes when he heard his phone ring, even before his alarm went off. What Sam had said had kept him awake for a long time the previous night. *Damn. how did I miss putting it on silent? Someone has woken up early in the morning with an agenda just to wake me up*. He tapped under his pillow, searching for his mobile phone. His vision was blurry as he read 'Victor calling'. He jumped off the bed when rubbed his eyes and looked at the name clearly. His eyes instantly shuffled to the time on top of the screen which read 06:14 am. Andrew frowned. *Why?* He stared at the screen dwelling in his thoughts before attending the call.

'Sir?' he whispered with a morning voice.

'Andrew. Sorry to disturb you at this time,' Victor panted.

'That's not a problem, sir. What happened?'

'Sam. We couldn't find her at home. I searched thoroughly in and around the house. I couldn't think of any other places.' He sighed. 'We need your help. Please!'

Andrew was baffled. He recalled Victor's call six months back, nearly a repeat of this conversation. *I wonder if I had made her life any better.* His impulsive thought rang in his head for a second.

'Andrew. Are you there?' Victor said over the silence from the other side.

'Yes, sorry. I'm going now. Don't panic. I'm sure she is around.'

Andrew hung up the call, dropping himself on the bed in shock. He lost grip on his thoughts while the scenes from the dormitory and the previous night ran through his head.

He rushed out of his apartment in his shorts and T-shirt. His face stayed frowned, and he counted numbers in reverse while he rode the bike.

CHAPTER 31

This part of my life went totally out of hand and it may be called Karma. I apparently did not take the usual route while running back home from the cemetery. I tripped upon my own foot and hit on a pole. The metal pole punctured my head starting from head to chin. My vision turned blurry and everything I looked began to swirl. I felt blood flowing from my cheekbone while I gradually fell unconscious.

Andrew went in search of me at possibly all the wrong places; not to complain, that was totally derived from his past experiences with me. He went to the old water tank building where I used to dwell in the world of hallucination; he went to the church, visited Varun's house, and searched all around the playground that was right at the corner of our street. He also visited the cemetery to check if I was at Bunny's grave and was distressed about my missing. He was saturated with the dismal rain drops one after the other, he then fell to his knees right outside the cemetery in utter hopelessness while I sopped in the muddy water in the middle of the road a street away from where he was.

I had the utmost desire to live at that moment when I was left to die in the middle of the road. According to Andrew's narrative: A dog was barking at him continuously before he could start from the cemetery, and he initially just ignored it. The dog seemed to chase him barking fiercely behind his vehicle. Andrew stopped to check if something was wrong with the dog and thought he could help him although he was devastated; that is Andrew precisely.

He realized he knew the dog: it was the one I used to feed every time I went to the church. He pleasingly asked Andrew to follow him, moving to and fro towards the street where I was collapsed with half of my body sopping in the rain. The rainwater flooded my nose almost blocking my breathing. Andrew sprinted to me, lifting my body in his arms letting the hands and legs lifelessly dangle as he ran. He desperately waited for several minutes for a vehicle to pass by. The vehicles only sped by faster due to the pouring rain. At last, he managed to stop an SUV by almost plunging in front of the car. He brought the dog along.

I don't believe in a single form of a god. I don't believe that if you sit and chant a thing desperately, you can simply achieve it. I don't think miracles can happen. But this happened to me. That day, I opened my eyes to the happiest faces of my mom and dad, which I desperately wished for before I fell unconscious. That made me recall the maths exam I got through, despite performing terribly. What do you think are these surreal chances that life randomly throws at us though we don't deserve them? Before I get to that, you should know what happened next. I have lived the happiest times of my life since that incident. Andrew and I had a dream wedding. My parents were delighted with our decision. Andrew and I started a charitable trust to give shelter and food to the unfortunate. I was also pregnant within a year of the marriage.

Life randomly throws second chances at us though we don't deserve them; these are the chances to correct the mistakes we made in the past. If the mistakes are irreversible, these are the chances to serve Karma. I was blessed with a baby boy. I delivered him in spite of warnings from the doctors that it would be life-threatening for me. I survived six days after the birth of my son. Over the third day, I realized that he totally resembled Simon and that that was my chance to pay him back. But the universe did what it has to do.

I know that these are my final days. People just know that; no death is a surprise to the one who dies. I'm sure Simon knew that it was going to be his last day. All he wanted was for me not to lose. Little did he know, that even after three years of his passing, he won over me; I did lose again; gloriously. My son surely is in the best hands he could ever wish for.

* * *

If you enjoyed this book, please take a few moments to write a review of it on Amazon. Thank you!

www.ingramcontent.com/pod-product-compliance
Lightning Source LLC
LaVergne TN
LVHW041025150826
845672LV00001B/203

* 9 7 9 8 8 9 0 2 6 8 2 8 0 *